Grim Hunter Collection

Volume 1

by Suzanne Fisher

Table of Contents

Forward

The Grim series has a long and nostalgic history for me. These four stories constitute, in a very real sense, a discrete chapter in my original (as opposed to fanfiction) story-writing career.

A decade ago, I wrote these four stories for an online "boys-love" webzine. I wrote them under a pseudonym, following the theme of the webzine each month.

At the time, I'd never done anything quite like this. I'd noodled around with novel-length works, and I'd written a lot of short-works in other people's sandboxes, but I hadn't written a lot of short works where I had to introduce the characters and world on my own. I decided to write a series of stories, instead of standalone ones, and they were pretty well-received.

I stopped writing for the webzine, and it fell into obscurity, but James and Sebastian never really faded into the depths of my brain. I always enjoyed writing in their universe, and I slowly began to develop further stories in their universe. Their storyline developed more depth and their universe got bigger. But these foundational stories are still some of my favourites, though there are flaws I see now, that I never considered so many years ago.

I think they're a solid introduction, though, and I hope that whatever you think of them, that you enjoy them for what they are - an introduction to a universe that definitely has romance, but where there's a lot more going on than it might first seem.

I hope you enjoy these first stories, and look forward to the next ones.

A Grim Disguise

Marseilles was a beautiful city, though like many European cities, it subscribed to the 'densely packed' school of architecture. The stone buildings practically climbed on top of each other as they marched up the sides of the hill that the city was built into, and the roads were so narrow and parking at such a premium, that most people drove their little cars up onto the sidewalks to park.

Those few who had cars in working condition, that was. Petrol was hard to find these days - as James well knew - and working car parts even more so. There were many vehicles that looked to have been abandoned in place for years, if not centuries. Rusting hulks barely recognizable anymore as vehicles hunched in place on the sidewalks, slowly flaking apart.

At this time of night, the roads were virtually empty, but the cobblestones and cracks in the road made it impossible for him to open up his motorcycle and go quickly. As a result, James was forced to take in a lot of the sights, whether he wanted to or not.

Closer to the water, things widened out a bit and he was able to speed up, the purr of the engine practically swallowed by the susurration of the sea. The famous Old Port was a wide harbour filled with little boats and bordered with a quaint boulevard. Presiding over the mouth of the port, on a spit of land that extended out into the Mediterranean Sea, was a smallish castle-like building, though James happened to know it was actually a fort.

Someone had taken up residence there. As James passed by the area on his way to the local police headquarters where his contact was supposed to be, he saw that several of the windows were lit with what looked like the warm glow of lamplight.

Perhaps that was the reason why there were hardly any people on the streets. Those who were out now, after sunset, moved with a rapid pace and furtive, frightened expressions. But James Grim scarcely noticed the oppressive weight of fear that had settled on the ancient city - he was too used to it.

No one ever invited a vampire hunter to a town that didn't have a vampire, after all.

There was a single lamp hung outside the door to the police station, the flame dancing merrily inside its glass cage. It could have been seen as a beacon of welcome to the city's saviour, but James saw its more practical purpose as he knocked on the heavy steel door and a small metal trapdoor slid aside to reveal one frightened brown eye.

It was there so they'd be able to see his face.

"Sorry!" the voice said, muffled by the intervening door. "We're not open right now." James tilted his hat back slightly so the man on the other side could see his face, too pale, angular, framed with black hair and set with startling blue eyes. "The names James Grim," he said. "I was sent." His French was articulate, but accented from his British heritage.

Clearly he was understood, though, because the eye widened fractionally and the window was shut with a clang. James folded his arms and waited, listening as the heavy bolts were slid aside before the door swung open. A painfully young-looking police constable regarded him for a moment. "Um, you're the hunter?" he asked nervously.

"I don't carry the stakes and silver knife for nothing," Grim replied. "Aren't you going to invite me in?"

The young man ducked his head and stepped back. "O-of course, please come in."

James smiled and stepped into the lobby area, removing his wide-brimmed hat and shaking out his long black hair, before looking up and glancing around. There were only two other people in the room besides him - the constable who'd let him in, and a middle-aged heavy-set man with the uniform of a highly-placed officer.

"Police Chief Doucette, I presume?" Grim asked, stepping forward with a faint smile to shake the officer's hand.

It was then that they saw his fangs.

The police chief recoiled, crossing himself and exclaiming a plea to God in French that made Grim's ears smart. The young constable had his gun out and was pointing it at Grim, the hand shaking badly enough the vampire was quite certain he wouldn't hit anything important even if he was foolhardy enough to fire.

Unfortunately, James wasn't surprised by the reaction. The vampire held the chief's gaze for a moment, and then glanced at the constable out of the corner of his eye. "Put that away, boy," he said. "I'm here to help your stupid ass, and all you'll do if you fire that thing is put a hole in my coat. And I *will* make you buy me a new one." The long leather duster was custom made, and it hadn't come cheap.

There was silence for a moment before Doucette nodded fractionally. "Put it away, Jacques," he said, his voice rasping.

Grim watched as the young man clicked the safety back on and, trembling, put the gun back in the holster at his hip. Then he turned his head and met Doucette's gaze again. "Glad that's out of the way. Tell me about the vampire problem."

Doucette swallowed. "The Vatican really sent you?" he asked suspiciously. "This is...not...acceptable."

Grim rolled his eyes and stuck a hand in his inside pocket - one of many - and he pulled out a square plastic card. "You want proof?" he asked, holding the card out to the man. "My visa, issued by our Mother the Holy Church."

Doucette hesitated, then took the card and picked up a reader on the desk behind him. In a moment he'd swiped it and was looking over the data on the screen. "James Alexander Grim," he read aloud. "The passport is in order."

"But it can't be you!" Jacques burst out. "We need someone else!"

"Look," James snapped, turning his glare on the young man. "Yes, I'm a vampire - all the better to kill the monsters with, my dear. What do you care how they die, so long as they're dead? I'll be out of town before you know it."

"That's not the issue, Monsieur Grim," Doucette said quietly. He seemed to have regained his calm and as he held out James' card to return it, his hand didn't tremble.

"What's the issue, then?" James asked. "We're burning darkness, sir, and I doubt you people have time to wait for the Vatican to send a replacement."

"There is no issue," Doucette said, shooting a glare at the younger man. "I think the young man is merely hoping you can take care of things quickly and that you do not linger in our city too long."

"Like I said, that's the plan," Grim growled. He sensed there was something here that he was missing, but he was getting impatient with these people. "Look, just tell me what I need to know so I can put my back to this city. It'll make you happy, and it'll make *me* happy, and everyone can be happy. Okay?"

There was a moment of silence, and then the police chief nodded fractionally. "Okay." He straightened slightly, clasping his hands behind his back. "The vampire, who calls herself Lady Gwenhwyfar the Beautiful, has taken over Fort St. Jean, which you will see at the mouth of the Old Port. She's been...infecting many people. We don't know how many vampires are in there now, but perhaps a dozen?"

"A dozen vampires, inside a fortified castle," James said wryly. "Sounds like fun. No wonder everyone's hunkering in their houses like the plague has come. What about the zombies? How are your cemeteries?"

Vampirism was a disease - a sexually transmitted one. But it didn't just make people photosensitive and crave blood. That was if you were lucky.

If you were *really* lucky, you just got bitten and survived the experience. You might have a few days of fever and mild sensitivity to light. A good priest could drive it off in a couple of hours. If not, you could wait it out and hope you didn't get hit by a bus before it worked its way out of your system.

If you were mildly fortunate, you got a taste of the vampire's blood and fully contracted the disease. You'd live out the rest of your - exceptionally long - life as a monster, but at least you would *have* a life, and a will of your own. That's what had happened to James Grim some time ago.

Many people, especially those who encountered the real monsters - the vampires so heinous in their crimes that Grim was sent to kill them - were not so fortunate. They died with the disease-laced saliva or blood still in their system.

Usually such people were burned when their bodies were found, but sometimes the symptoms weren't recognized in time, or the body was left somewhere remote and not discovered. Those people became monsters of a different type. Mindless and vicious, the creatures still craved blood, but unlike vampires, were immune to pain. They'd attack until literally dismembered, and even then might manage to regenerate given enough time. The only way to stop a zombie permanently was to burn them to ashes.

At Grim's question, the chief went a little pale and swallowed. "There have been a few, but most have been caught and burned before they rose again," he said hollowly. "Gwenhwyfar has been kidnapping most of her victims and keeping them at the fort. Some of her progeny have been less careful."

James started, his eyes widening. "So there might be people still kept captive at the fort?" he asked. In that case, there wasn't any time to lose. Between a quickly growing army of vampires and the captives who could be added to their ranks at any moment, no wonder the city had called for help. What was actually surprising was that the city wasn't devastated already, given the math.

One thing was sure, though: sooner or later, this Gwenhwyfar would unleash her vampires on the city and it would be a right bloody mess.

Literally.

The chief nodded, though without much certainty. "There's no way to know, but I pray to God that some of them are still alive," he said, crossing himself again.

James winced and looked away at the gesture. Most people couldn't produce that kind of reaction with a simple movement of their hands, but when it was backed with real faith, even something so small packed a punch. Clearly he had a believer on his hands. Good thing they were on the same side.

"God doesn't have much to do with it," he growled. It was time to go. "I'll go take care of it." He turned away, placing his hat on his head again as he started for the door.

"Monsieur Grim," Doucette called after him, a hesitant note in his tone. "How are you going to get in?"

James paused, his hand on the door handle, and glanced over his shoulder. "What difference does it make to you?" he asked frankly.

Doucette blinked, taken aback. "I...I just mean, it may be difficult," he said awkwardly. "It's a fort, and you're a man -- by which I mean to say, just one man. The rumours of your prowess are impressive, but how can you storm a castle by yourself? The Lady doesn't take just any visitor."

James shook his head faintly, opening the door. "I don't expect you care much, chief," he said. "But vampires have a...camaraderie. She won't turn away a fellow monster at the door. Now are you going to let me go take care of your problem, or keep asking questions all night?" he added in an annoyed hiss.

There was a pause. "I'm sure you know better than I, Monsieur Grim."

"Yes," James said, striding through the door into the night. "I do."

* * *

Getting to the castle took only a few minutes. Dawn was still a while away, though it was later than James was comfortable with. Of course, once he got inside he would have lots of time to scope out the place before things got ugly.

The smell of brine and fish was strong in his nostrils as he parked his bike and continued up the slight rise to the fort proper. It was roughly square, with high stone walls and a single squat tower in one corner. Arrow slits glared at him like baleful eyes as he walked up to the heavy banded oak door and knocked.

He was sort of expecting the two double-barrelled shotguns that were shoved in his face as the door opened. What he wasn't expecting was the two blond women holding them. Both were dressed in voluminous dresses with multiple petticoats and necklines that left little to the imagination. Jewellery glittered at their throats and ears. Bracelets clinked against the stocks of the shotguns as they swung the barrels up.

James stuck his hands casually in his pockets as the door opened and outwardly pretended the guns weren't there even as he secretly grasped the handles of two silver throwing knives strapped to his thighs.

When he spoke, his British accent was gone, replaced by a vaguely Eastern European accent that wasn't specifically identifiable as being from any one region. "Is the lady of the castle home? I am the Baron von Liechtenstein. Perhaps you've heard of me." He smiled, showing off the points of his fangs.

The guns didn't waver. "You're not welcome here," one of the women hissed, her own fangs showing prominently, and in a much less friendly fashion.

Now that *was* a little shocking, and James actually found himself reacting like a real visiting Baron might. He recoiled slightly, his expression darkening as he hissed like a cat. "You dare to offend a visiting member of the family?" he exclaimed. "I come here, claiming right of hospitality. You can't refuse!"

This was unheard of, and actually quite frightening. One of the few things that *kept* vampires in check was how damn *predictable* they were. They loved nobility, gentility, manners. The fact that they were bloodthirsty menaces to society was something vampires almost tried to hide from one another.

The fact that there was a vampire who was not only massing an army, but apparently flaunting all of the conventions, made Grim's blood run cold.

"This gun is loaded with blessed silver pellets," the woman said triumphantly. "And the Lady Gwenhwyfar the Beautiful does not permit men in her castle. Get out of our territory Baron. Now!"

Doesn't permit MEN in her castle? Grim thought in confusion. "What the--"

The snick of crossbows being cocked reached his ears and he glanced up, seeing the wicked points of wood-shafted bolts poking out of the arrow slits all around him. Two more women were perched on the parapet above him, shotguns in their hands.

He counted at least eight weapons being pointed straight at him, and any one of them actually could really hurt, if not leave him dead. And every person he could see was unmistakeably a woman.

He drew his hands from his pockets, leaving the silver knives he'd been holding in their sheaths, and raised them in a conciliatory gesture. His smile felt pasted on. "Well then, my mistake," he said, backing away slowly. "Obviously I was unaware of the Lady's...preferences. Please send her my regards."

"Like I said," continued the speaker. "Lady Gwenhwyfar doesn't like men. You're better off just getting out of town, and telling anyone else who might want to come knocking, too."

"I'll be sure to do so," Grim replied. As he backed off, the door was shut tight, and he heard the unmistakeable sound of a bar settling into place. The women on the battlement remained in place, watching as he got back on his motorcycle. Swearing under his breath, he gunned the engine and headed back up the boulevard towards the police station.

Ten minutes later he was hammering on the door, and he'd worked himself up into a righteous lather. "Open up!" he shouted, uncaring of who might hear. "It's James Grim! Doucette, you frog bastard, let me in!"

He heard the bolts being thrown and left off banging on the door, noting with pleasure that he'd left a dent in the steel. Served them right.

Doucette opened the door a crack, but Grim was tired of playing games. One good shove and the Frenchman was stumbling backwards as James stepped inside.

"Go ahead," Grim challenged him, kicking the door closed so that it slammed. "Lie to me. Tell me you didn't know I was going to make a fool of myself."

Doucette's retreat was blocked by a desk and he put his hands back, leaning on them as if a few extra inches would save him. Grim stepped straight up to him and poked him in the chest with one long finger, looming over the shorter man.

Jacques was still there, as well. He sat at another desk like a statue, petrified.

"I...I tried to tell you..." Doucette began.

"You didn't try hard enough," James growled. "Do you think this is some kind of game?" His point made, he backed off a step from the red-faced man, folding his arms.

Doucette coughed, trying to pull himself together. He straightened his uniform, casting quick, nervous glances at Grim as if afraid the vampire was going to attack.

Grim glowered at him and let him worry.

"My apologies, Monsieur Grim," Doucette said when he'd straightened himself out. "I meant to tell you, but you seemed to be in a hurry. I hoped you would be able to succeed even though you're not the...best candidate."

James sighed. "You were afraid I'd leave," he said bluntly. He rubbed his eyes, the anger fleeing and replaced with resignation. "Give me something to write on."

With a perplexed frown, Doucette tore a sheet of paper from a notepad and passed it to the taller man along with a pen. James found himself a clear surface and started scribbling a quick list of items.

"You a married man, Monsieur Doucette?" he asked as he pondered the list and added a few more items in his quick, angular hand.

Doucette started in surprise. "Ah...yes, I am," he said warily, unconsciously rubbing the gold band on his finger.

"Good," James said. "If you want me to stay, it'll cost you an additional 500 Euros, plus the cost of getting me the items on this list." He handed the page back to the policeman. "Have your wife get me these things today. I'll be back at dusk. Now the night is wasted and I have to find a place to sleep for the day."

Doucette's eyes bugged out as he scanned the list. "Are you mad?" he exclaimed, looking up to meet Grim's determined gaze. "This'll never work."

"It better work," James replied, starting for the door. "Because whatever this bitch is building an army for, I don't think it's going to wait for another hunter to arrive from Rome."

* * *

It had been an exercise in frustration and humiliation, but by the time the clock was tolling midnight, James Grim was being driven up to Fort St. John in a horse-drawn carriage. A yawning Jacques was at the reins, dressed in livery and looking quite smart, albeit with dark circles under his eyes from being kept up all last night and the day following.

Turned out he was the only constable still left in town, as Gwen's bitches had been targeting anyone in uniform for a quick death, which was why he wasn't getting much sleep lately. Learning that had made James revise his opinion of the kid upwards a few notches.

The door to the castle was open by the time the carriage came to a full stop. Two women - only one of whom James recognized, as one of the ones who'd been standing on the parapet with a shotgun in her hands - emerged from the doorway. They were still holding their guns but this time kept them pointed at the ground.

Jacques cleared his throat nervously and announced loudly. "Introducing her ladyship the Baroness von Liechtenstein here to beg the hospitality of Lady Gwenhwyfar the Beautiful."

He jumped down and hurried to the door of the carriage just as James opened it, reaching up to help him down.

And it was help he sorely needed.

James reached out as delicately as he could and grasped Jacques' hand as he desperately tried to rearrange the voluminous skirts, petticoats and the hem of his travelling cloak so he could step down without tripping and killing himself. He felt the ridiculous pointed shoes wobble a little on the first step and heard Jacques whimper as he squeezed his hand hard.

He forced himself to loosen his grip, wincing a little as he imagined the bruise the man would probably have. Then he was safely on the ground and moved up the walk, throwing his hood back.

Madame Doucette had taken to the project like a duck to water, and had made some major alterations to James' appearance. His fall of long black hair had been transformed into a thick mass of ringlets. His dress was cut high enough not to reveal cleavage he didn't possess, and both he and Monsieur Doucette had been shocked to learn that women had silicone inserts in their undergarments to provide some added volume to their busts. Four sets of those and even James was filling out his bustier nicely.

All in all, she'd spent two hours coifing, primping, shaving, plucking and painting until he was virtually unrecognizable even to himself.

The hardest part had been finding shoes that would fit. In the end, Madame Doucette had stuffed him into a pair he insisted were still a size too small and told him he'd have to live with it.

As he stepped away from Jacques and toward the women at the door, James caught a glimpse of the young man tugging his high collar up a little further, as if ensuring bite marks were hidden. With the deathly pallor caused by fear and the black circles under his eyes, Jacques was the picture of a vampire's servant whose Mistress took little care with her toys.

Good boy, Grim thought. Now if only the rest of this complex operation could go equally well.

James minced up the walk, holding his skirts up out of the dirt and trying not to break his ankle on any of the myriad cracks in the flagstones.

As the Baron, Grim had given his voice a subtle accent, just enough to carry the part. This time when he opened his mouth, his r's rolled like the sea, his th's were firmly z's and his voice fluttered like a bird.

All the better to distract from the fact that he was straining his voice just to hit a more feminine pitch.

"Please take me to yourrrr mistress," he trilled, drawing out the words as if afraid to let them escape their cages. "I have had ze *most* drrrrreadful trip and simply *must* rrrrrest my bones."

There was a choked sound from Jacques, but the young man quickly gathered up the reins and turned the carriage towards town before it could turn into full-blown laughter.

Yuk it up, bloodsack, Grim thought with an inward glower.

The two women exchanged incredulous glances, then looked at Grim cautiously. "There was a Baron von Liechtenstein who came to our door yesterday--"

James was ready with his answering salvo - in fact, he'd chosen his persona and nome de plume with it in mind. He raised a hand in a silencing gesture. "Speak to me not of zat horrrrrible man. He treated me badly - very badly. I do not vish to sink of him! I'm sure he came to you in ze hopes zat I would take him back ven I arrived."

He narrowed his gaze. "You did not let him in, did you? I had hoped zis vould be a safe haven for me, avay from ze man-pigs!"

"Oh no," one of the women said hastily, and she actually came out to James and took his arm to lead him inside. "You've definitely come to the right place. What did he do, Baroness?" she asked with great sympathy. The other woman had disappeared - probably racing ahead to prepare the mistress of the house for her guest.

James produced a lace handkerchief and sniffled into it artistically. He felt foolish, and couldn't believe they were falling for it. "I do not vish to dwell on my shame, but I tell you zis - if I never have to see or touch a man again, it vill be too soon!"

The woman made sympathetic noises and a moment later they stepped from the rather dark hallway into an open, high-ceilinged room that might have started life as the Fort's mess hall. Now it was decorated from floor to ceiling and hung with blazing chandeliers.

A woman sat in a high-backed chair at one end, attended by half a dozen women who sat in smaller chairs or reclined on cushions on the floor. The woman was frankly beautiful, her hair a mass of golden curls, her body slim and narrow-waisted. Her skin had the ethereal porcelain colour of a vampire who kept herself well-fed.

She rose from her chair and approached James, who noted with surprise that she was nearly as tall as he was. "Baroness, I am Lady Gwenhwyfar, mistress of this castle. I bid you welcome here."

Her accent was English, reminiscent of queens, but Grim's instincts told him it was as fake as the accent he was using at the moment.

James curtseyed as best he could. "It is my honour to accept your hospitality, Lady Gwenhwyfarrrr."

Gwen closed the distance between them, extending her arms. For a horrible moment, James thought she was going to hug him, but she just took his hands.

"You poor dear," she said. "Fleur told me of your harrowing journey from...Liechtenstein. What, pray, brought you to Marseilles in the first place?"

James took a small step away from the woman. It was subtle, but he'd grown up in London and knew what they sounded like. He would bet his motorcycle the woman had been born and bred in Marseilles. Why was she pretending to be a British queen, surrounding herself with pretty vampire girls and hiding in this castle like a fairytale princess?

Even as his quick mind took in and analyzed the various observations, James continued to spin his tale. "My husband and I have been married a c-century," he said, hiding his face in the handkerchief again and allowing his voice to tremble. "We thought a second honeymoon would rekindle ze spark, so we came to wine country, but before we arrived, I learned..." He shuddered to a stop dramatically.

Gwenhwyfar took his hand again and squeezed. "There, there," she said. "I understand, you needn't finish. Men are not worthy of us!" She glanced around, snapping her fingers. Several women hurried out of the room and another one rose from a cushion and approached.

"You must be exhausted. You can rest here as long as you like, Baroness. Do you like Samantha, here?"

Startled by the question, James looked up and met the frightened blue eyes of yet another blond.

This one was human.

Gwen put a possessive arm around the woman's shoulders. She was young, scarcely more than a girl, and there were healing marks on her swan-like neck. Next to the tall Gwenhwyfar, she looked even smaller and younger. Fragile.

"Take her," Gwen urged gently, drawing the girl closer to James. "She will refresh you. Just please do me the favour of leaving her alive. I wish to turn her when she's ready."

Samantha shuddered and James felt his stomach twist in sympathy.

"Thank you," he heard himself say, reaching out to take the girl's hand. "You are too kind, Lady Gwenhwyfar."

Gwen bowed deeply. "I know you'll take good care of her. If you follow Jeannette, she will show you to your room."

The first thing he saw when he entered the room they'd prepared for him was a four-poster bed hung with sheer curtains. In fact, there was no other furniture beyond that, other than a sideboard with a sink.

He released Samantha's hand the instant the door closed and glanced around to try to get his bearings. He was on the second floor, and on the side looking out over the Mediterranean. The smell of the sea wafting through his window was strong, and not unpleasant.

So far he'd counted at least a dozen vamps in the place. How many more could there be? Even though they were probably all brand new vampires, unused to their new power, this wasn't going to be easy. He'd probably have to wait until dawn to start his investigation of the place.

He was aware of Samantha as she moved to the bed and curled up on it, her legs drawn up to her chest and her skirts disarranged. James' eyes were drawn to her ankles despite himself. They were slim and shapely, and she wore some kind of slippers that looked a lot more comfortable than the torture devices he had on his own feet.

He felt himself start to salivate and he looked away, glaring out the window. It had been a long time - he'd been expecting to feed the night before, and now the urge was starting to become acute.

All right, time to get some information.

He turned towards the girl and crossed the room, sitting on the bed. "Samantha?" he said. "How long have you been here?" How badly had she been used? Some people, when held by vampires for a long time, came to love their captors. Grim had never understood why, but there was every chance that she'd betray his mission to her mistresses, instead of wanting to be rescued.

She looked up, and confusion warred for a moment with the nervousness in her eyes. "Two weeks," she said softly. "Why do you ask?"

James considered her for a moment. "I only wonder how eager you are to be brought into the fold. Is the Lady good to you?"

Samantha was silent for a moment, her gaze growing furtive and uncertain, rather than outright frightened. "What are you really here for, monsieur?" she asked suddenly, her voice pitched in a whisper.

James started, his eyes widening in shock. "W-what did you say?" he exclaimed, his voice cracking as he belatedly tried to hit the upper register.

The girl smiled triumphantly, though her eyes were still wary. "I knew it. You cover your throat, and I'll bet you anything vampires hardly *ever* do that, do they? Only Gwenhwyfar does. Your voice sounds funny. And you smell of gun oil."

"I do not," James hissed, his mind racing. He was sure he'd fooled them; how had she had figured it out?

But something Samantha had said caught at his mind and he raised a hand to the silk scarf wrapped around his neck. It had been a difficult decision, but he'd had to do something to cover his Adam's apple or the whole ruse would have been for nothing.

James had never seen a vampire cover their throat. Only their servants did that, to hide the puncture marks; it would be like a queen putting on jewellery made of gold-painted plastic and glass.

But now that he thought about it, Gwenhwyfar had been wearing a dress with a high neckline that covered her throat.

He looked at Samantha and saw her lips curve in a knowing grin. "Gwenhwyfar is a man?" he asked incredulously.

"Yes, monsieur," Samantha said. She swallowed, the smirk faltering. "Why are you here?"

James was still trying to wrap his mind around the fact that Gwen was not only a fake limey, but a man, too. *Next she's going to tell me Gwen's not really a vampire.*

He wrenched his mind back around to Samantha's question after a moment, however. Those cornflower blue eyes were searching his expression and he'd already learned how discerning they were. Besides, what did he care what equipment Gwen had between her - his - legs? She'd still burn.

James kicked off his shoes and felt his feet throb with relief, but didn't take any time to enjoy it. He reached for Samantha and drew her closer, feeling her stiffen as he put his lips near her ear. They'd already said enough that he was pretty sure no one had been listening at the door up to this point, but for all he knew some spy could come by at any moment to check on them.

Better to make sure - and get her used to the position at the same time.

"My name is James Grim. I'm a vampire hunter. I'm here to kill every vampire in this place," he said. Samantha started in his arms and relaxed slightly.

"Thank God," she whispered. There was just enough real faith in the word that it made James flinch slightly. "Thank you, monsieur," she added quickly.

"How many other prisoners are there?" James asked. He could hear the rush of blood in her veins, but held himself tightly in check. "How many left alive?"

Samantha swallowed. "Just me," she said. "I'm the only one. Gwenhwyfar said...to stop taking prisoners. She said she had enough to rule this city now."

"That's her goal? To rule Marseilles?" James asked. His nostrils flared - how good she smelled. Her heart was beating rapidly, fluttering under her breast like a trapped bird.

She pressed her forehead to his shoulder and nodded. As he held her, her body was relaxing slowly in his arms, though he could still feel her nervousness.

"That's fine," James said softly. "I'll stop her, but you've got to help me, Samantha."

She looked up, her eyes wide. "Sure," she said eagerly. "Of course. What do you want me to do?"

"Don't struggle," Grim whispered, curling a hand in her hair and tilting her head back to bare her throat.

She froze for an instant, then cried out, the sound high with terror. "Wait, wait stop!" she exclaimed, pushing at his chest with her small hands. A short string of German escaped her lips, and while James spoke only a dozen words or so of the language, it was enough to recognize that she was swearing.

He paused, surprised enough by that to do so. "Look, Samantha--" he began harshly, but she wasn't listening to him.

"Please, don't bite me," she said, her voice breathless with renewed terror. "I can help you in other ways. Please give me a chance!"

There was nothing for it - James *needed* to feed, and if he couldn't feed from her, the desire would eventually overcome him at the worst possible time. At least Samantha was probably already infected and would be in no additional danger from him. In a week or two she'd be out of the woods, regardless of what he did now. This was the way he'd fed his hunger for centuries - from the victims of the vampires he killed.

Some called him a monster for victimizing someone who'd already been through so much, but he figured it at least stopped him from having to hunt on the streets. He'd done that for long enough.

"What can you do?" he asked anyway, his voice tight with need. He needed to get her to calm down. In his current state of hunger, if she struggled while he drank and awakened his hunting instincts, he could easily kill her by accident.

"Lots of things," she said, clenching her fists in his loose, puffy sleeves. "I'm...I'm not what I seem, monsieur. I..." She swallowed. "I'll show you."

Suddenly her body *shifted* under Grim's hands. It was the most bizarre thing he'd ever felt in his life. Her hips narrowed and breasts shrank, reshaping themselves like putty. Her face widened and grew less delicate. Her blonde hair darkened to a less golden colour closer to straw and her blue eyes shifted towards the grey of storm clouds.

James jerked his hands away, repulsed by the sensation. In less than ten seconds the girl was a boy, still young and delicate-looking, but rounder of face. He looked to be perhaps sixteen, still smooth-cheeked but starting to show signs of growing into a man. His hair was straight and chopped off unevenly rather than coiled into tight ringlets, and he no longer quite fit the dress. It hung wrongly off of his flat chest and strained at his waist.

"My name is Sebastian," he said softly. Even his voice was different - still youthful, but deeper than before, and James had to revise his estimation of his age upwards a notch. He was a young man, smaller than James, but an adult, barely. "I had to pretend to be a girl or the vampires would have killed me. Sir, I've lived on the streets since I was young. I can get in and out of anywhere. I can hide and sneak. And I'm *supposed* to be here. I'm sure there's something I can do to help."

James stared at him. "Is *anyone* in this damned building a woman?" he demanded, a bit louder than he'd intended. He immediately clamped his mouth shut, cursing inwardly, and continued more softly. "You're a shape changer. I thought they were a myth."

"Shape shifter," Sebastian corrected, reaching up to scrub a hand through his hair, disarranging it even further. "And if it weren't for me being one, I'd think they were a myth, too. I've never met anyone else like me." He looked at James warily through the curtain formed by his hair. "Well? Are you going to help me out of here?"

"Of course I am," James said dismissively. Shape shifters...now that was a new one. They were so rare that he'd never met one - that he was aware of. People called them monsters, but so far as he knew they didn't hurt humans - no more than other humans did, anyway. People were mostly afraid of them because they could look like anyone they wanted.

Apparently they could even change their own gender.

Sebastian looked immensely relieved and broke into a brilliant and somewhat lopsided smile. "Thank you, monsieur," he said fervently. "What do you want me to do?"

James sighed and reached out, curling a hand in the collar of the dress and dragging Sebastian against him again. The boy gasped softly and stiffened, putting his hands against James' chest to keep their bodies separate a few inches. "I want you not to struggle, pup," he said. "Boy or girl, I still need blood. I'm a vampire, and you say you're the only person available."

"But..." Sebastian's good mood evaporated in an instant and he trembled, straining against James' grasp. "I don't understand. You're supposed to be *rescuing* me. I...This isn't right..."

"It's not about what's right or wrong, kid," Grim murmured. "It's about what I need in order to do what I have to do. Or would you rather I had picked out some random person on the street before I came here tonight?"

Sebastian was silent for a moment. "No," he said softly. "I wouldn't rather that." The trembling eased slightly and he grew more pliant in James' arms.

"This is really what you need? That's...the only reason you're doing it?"

"I'm a vampire, kid," Grim said, and sank his teeth into Sebastian's throat.

The boy gasped and whimpered softly, his fingers fisting against Grim's chest. Sweet red blood flowed into James' mouth and he drank it down greedily. There was a unique flavour to the blood and he wondered if it was because Sebastian was a shape shifter. It...sparkled against his tongue, like nothing he'd ever tasted.

Sweet lord, it made him want more.

The caution, the desire not to truly hurt the fragile creature in his arms beyond repair, flew straight out of his mind. James tightened his grip with a moan and pressed closer, swallowing each pulse of sweet nectar that flowed over his tongue.

He heard a cry of fear, but that only made the taste sweeter.

The heartbeat thundered in Grim's ears and he shifted his leg over the boy, baring a stockinged knee in a rustle of petticoats. There was far too much fabric, but Grim was beyond caring. There was bare skin under his lips and blood in his mouth, and that was all he cared about.

Suddenly he felt the boy start to shift, but as he didn't seem to be trying to get away, James only registered it distantly. A hand pushed fabric aside and slid upwards until it rubbed against James' groin.

Even in James' current state, he started at the unexpected sensation. But discouraging the boy never entered his mind. He growled softly against Sebastian's throat and rocked his hips forward a little, feeling his body react. He was sheathed in the nylon from hips to toes, but it did nothing to dull the sensation, and the scanty underwear Madame Doucette had made him wear 'for shape' did even less.

The silk of the underpants slid over his cock as Sebastian rubbed with his palm, and James grew hard quickly. Sebastian rubbed faster, the slowly building rhythm sending waves of pleasure through James' body that enhanced the sweet flavour of the blood that flowed over his tongue.

James freed a hand and delved lower. Somewhere in his mind was the thought that he should return the favour. No one had ever seemed to...*enjoy* this before, and while he could scarcely think through the pure pleasure of this feeding, some instinctive part of him liked that Sebastian seemed to be getting into it.

After spending an eternity pushing fabric aside, his fingers brushed the inside of Sebastian's thigh and the join of his legs. The boy was soft and James started to rub with the heel of his hand, the same way Sebastian was, allowing the silk of the underwear to stimulate the boy's member as much as the pressure of his hand did.

Suddenly the hand left his own groin and he groaned, the sound shading towards a growl as he was left bereft.

"N-no," Sebastian whispered, his voice thready. He curled his small hand around Grim's wrist and pulled him away. "Please just...just let me..."

Frowning, James pulled his fangs from Sebastian's throat. Blood welled up and he licked it away, unable to resist the pull of it. "What are you--" the question was cut off by a heartfelt moan as

Sebastian's hand resumed its rubbing. The scanty underwear was stretched tight by his erection and his cock throbbed as if with the beat of a heart.

There was no response from Sebastian and James was too distracted to press the matter. James closed his eyes and felt the sensations spiral through his body, growing heightened as the boy masturbated him faster and faster.

His tongue flicked out every few seconds, just to get another taste of that heady elixir that leaked from Sebastian's throat, but the wounds were closing and the flow was lessening to a trickle.

A few timeless moments later, James shuddered and spilled himself over Sebastian's hand. The orgasm pulled his mouth away from Sebastian's neck and he rolled onto his back as he arched upwards, lost in the ecstasy.

The boy pulled his hand back, watching him solemnly, his chest heaving as he pressed his hand to the wounds on his neck. When James finally collected himself enough to look at him, he saw renewed wariness in the boy's eyes. "Are you done?" Sebastian asked.

Realization hit James like a thunderbolt.

"Does this happen every time someone bites you?" he asked, pushing himself up to sit.

Sebastian slipped off the bed and moved to the basin, washing his soiled hands. He didn't *quite* take his eyes off of Grim. "Does what happen?"

It occurred to James that Sebastian probably wasn't as well acquainted with vampire bites as he was. He swung his feet over the side of the bed to the floor, but saw the boy tense up even from across the room and thought better of standing up.

"Kid, let me put it this way - I don't usually lose control like that. I was only planning to take a bit, but...Do the vamps always try to kill you?" James said frankly.

Sebastian dried his hands on a towel and then wadded it up and pressed it to the side of his neck. He did leave red spots on the towel, but vampire saliva - ironically enough - had healing properties, and he wasn't bleeding much.

If you could bottle the stuff, you'd make a mint. If anyone would be willing to buy it, anyway.

"Always," he said in a slightly haunted voice, his eyes sliding away to study a particularly interesting spot on the far wall. "Gwenhwyfar...she says she wants to make me a vampire. But every time she bites me, I have to do what I did to you...to distract her. That's how I know she's a man."

He glanced at James. "I'd rather die than be a vampire, monsieur. But I don't want to be a zombie, either."

James gave Sebastian a wry look. His blood had run cold at the thought of what the boy had been going through, but he didn't allow much of it to show on his face. "I understand, kid. But I can tell you that neither of those things is going to happen to you. You'll be back to your life sooner than you know it."

Sebastian's lips twisted wryly for some reason, but he didn't elaborate. "Thank you," he said, and the words were sincere enough. "Is there...anything I *can* do to help?" he added hopefully. "I mean besides donating blood."

"Just keep out of the way," James said with a sigh, shifting to lie back on the bed again. He needed to get some sleep, and felt pleasantly spent after the good feeding and...other things. "And don't blow my cover."

Sebastian glared at him. "Weren't you listening to me? I can do things!"

"Good," James said, raising his head enough to meet the glare. It was cute, but not terribly threatening. "Those skills will serve you well after I get you out of here. For now, get some rest. You look like you're about to fall over."

Indeed, the boy was pale as death, and swaying in place.

"I'll be okay," he said stubbornly, but moved slowly across the room to the bed. Casting a nervous glance at James, he stretched out on the mattress.

James was quite certain that if there'd been anything else to lie down on other than the bed, the kid would have taken it. He glanced at Sebastian briefly, and then deliberately closed his eyes and turned away. "I won't bite you again, kid. Relax."

Sebastian swallowed audibly. "Okay," he said softly.

And that was the last James Grim knew for a while, as he slipped into a satisfied sleep.

* * *

James awoke when the shutters on the window were closed with a bang and a rattle. His eyes snapped open and he stared up into the darkness for a few moments, getting his bearings again.

It was close to dawn. He could feel the lethargy setting in and sat up to combat it. All over the castle the vampires would be settling down to sleep, but this vampires wasn't about to surrender to unconsciousness for the day. He had work to do.

And Sebastian was gone.

The cold expanse of the bed where the boy had been laying gave James pause for a moment. *He wasn't kidding about being able to sneak,* he thought, impressed despite himself that the boy had managed to leave the room without waking James up.

Perhaps the blood had been partly to blame for how deeply he'd slept. Yeah, that explained it.

I just hope it doesn't hang him. Grim didn't have time to look for him, and if Sebastian was still in the castle when James' plan went off, he'd die with the vampires.

But there was nothing he could do. Hopefully the boy would find him before it was too late.

James squeezed his feet into the shoes again, ensured that nothing had shifted while he was asleep, and headed out of the room.

A few minutes later he was on the ground floor, working his way around the perimeter of the building. The whole place was shut up tight against the approaching dawn, every shutter closed and latched. Gwen had done a wonderful job of prettying up the place, with carpet runners in the hallways and wall hangings breaking up the cold drabness of the centuries-old stone.

That just made James smile as he put his plan into effect.

He reached into his dress, felt around and then pulled one of the silicone inserts out of his brassiere. A quick reach up his own skirt and he was able to pull the silver knife from the sheath strapped to his thigh. The whole operation would have looked quite odd to anyone watching, but of course there wasn't anyone around *to* watch.

He sliced open the insert and started squeezing the contents over the carpet and wall hangings. The smell of the lighter fluid he'd filled the things was thick in his nostrils.

He worked his way around, leaving a trail of the highly flammable liquid behind him. James had just started work on the fourth insert when he heard the sound of running feet coming towards him.

Shit! he thought, glancing around quickly for somewhere to hide what he was doing, but a door burst open nearby and Sebastian emerged from the stairwell at a full-out run.

James relaxed immediately, and was about to resume what he was doing, when he got a good look at the boy. Sebastian was female again, but his hair was dishevelled and his dress torn to reveal a bit more bosom than was probably decent.

"James!" Sebastian raced towards him, shifting to male form as he ran. His cheeks were pale and stained with tears.

The shift seemed to throw him off balance - perhaps he'd never shape-changed at a dead run before - and he tripped over his own feet as it completed. He fell headlong into James, who somehow managed to catch him without stabbing him with the knife.

"Hell kid, what the hell is wrong with you?" he demanded. "Where have you been?"

There didn't seem to be anyone chasing him, so why was he running as though some monster was at his heels? Why the tears?

"James, it...it happened," Sebastian said, then burst into tears, burying his face against Grim's chest and sobbing. "She called for me when you were asleep, and she made me drink her b-blood."

James felt himself go very still, his eyes widening. Of all the rotten luck.

He put his hands on the boy's shoulders and pushed him back gently, putting some space between them. The boy was shaking and his cheeks were reddened - of course, the fever set in quickly when you got a full dose of the infection. It was already starting.

"Sorry kid," James said in a detached voice. "Guess it didn't work out. You want me to make it quick? Your body will burn - it won't become a zombie."

Sebastian's grey eyes widened, the tears drying up in his shock. "W-what?" he gulped. "You...you're going to kill me now? I thought you were going to *save* me!"

James lowered his hands. "No one can save you now, kid," he said softly. "And I won't turn another monster on the world."

"I'm not a monster!" Sebastian shouted, and Grim winced at the volume. He took a step forward, intending to try to get him to be quiet, and the boy back-pedalled until his back hit the wall, a soft cry of terror coming to his throat. "Please!" he exclaimed, and thankfully he was softer this time. "Please give me a chance. I won't hurt people, I swear."

The door opened again and this time Gwenhwyfar emerged. She strode towards them, her head held high. "Samantha you naughty-- Samantha?"

Sebastian squeaked and inched away, caught. "Leave me alone!" he snapped.

Despite his earlier words, James stepped between them, the silver knife held loosely in his hand. "Lady Gwenhwyfar," he said, not even attempting to disguise his voice. "You should be in bed."

She - or he - stared at James, eyes widening. "B-Baroness you..." her voice trailed off, eyes going to James' chest, where he no longer filled out the bosom nearly so well, since most of the contents were now spattered over the floor.

"James Grim," he introduced himself, bowing slightly. "And you've made your last monster." He walked towards her, his steps deliberate. Maybe she'd run. That'd be interesting.

She took a step back, but didn't run, her fangs bared in a snarl. "You're a man," she hissed. "I hate men."

"*You* are a man," James said. He darted forward, closing the gap between them and grabbing her by the collar. She gasped as her back slammed against the nearest wall.

"I am not!" she exclaimed, beating at his arms. He winced at the hits, but held on. "It's only an accident of birth!"

Suddenly Grim felt a white-hot pain bury himself in his stomach. He gasped and his fingers loosened, allowing Gwenhwyfar to slide to the ground again.

She made a twisting motion and the knife she'd stabbed into his gun twisted, tearing the wound open further.

James staggered back, clutching at the knife handle with his free hand. He saw her advance, smirking, and felt a hard-toed stiletto shoe strike his knee, sending a shooting pain through his leg.

All right, he thought through the fog of pain. *That's it.*

He forced himself to straighten and shot out a leg, grunting as the movement sent another pulse of pain through his stomach. His boot slammed heavily into her groin and she crumpled to the floor, proving once and for all that Sebastian had been right about her physical gender.

Before she could recover, he bent and brought his silver knife down fast, stabbing her through the heart.

She shrieked and went limp, her head lolling to one side as she immediately began to dissolve into a pile of ash.

From the quickness of the reaction, she must have been several centuries old, and mad from it. They often were. And the older the vampire, the more quickly they turned to ash when shuffled off their immortal coil.

James turned towards Sebastian, who was still rooted to the spot, the boy's eyes wide as he watched Grim murder the creature who'd kept him captive. The boy caught his eye and took a step back, swallowing. "I won't be a monster," he insisted softly.

James extracted the knife from his stomach and threw it aside, pressing a hand to the wound. He was bleeding, but it'd heal. "You say that now," he said to

Sebastian, shaking his head. He fought to keep his voice even through the pain. "But it's different when you get hungry. When you can smell the blood. You saw me last night. You've seen what these women became."

"But *you* do it!" Sebastian pleaded. "You can be good. Why can't I? Please, monsieur. Please let me go. I swear to God that I won't be a monster."

The boy had something in his hand, his fingers clamped firmly around it. When he raised his hands in his plea, his hands opened and the silver cross dropped to dangle from its chain. James flinched back from the sight of it, though the reflex was weak.

He ground his teeth. "...All right," he said softly.

Sebastian jerked, taking a step towards the older man. "You mean it?" he gasped.

"Yeah," James said, turning away and moving to finish up the circuit. He had to get this done before the sun rose too high, anyway, or he himself wouldn't be able to escape. He limped on down the hall. "Get out of here, now, and leave the front door unlatched. But if I ever catch you preying on the innocent, I'll make your death nice and slow. Got it?"

"Yes," Sebastian said, and his voice was solemn. "Yes, I've got it."

He turned, starting off, and James called after him suddenly. "Hey kid." He watched as the boy turned in a swish of skirts, looking at him fearfully over his shoulder.

"You'll wish you took my offer, you know," James said. "A quick death here is better than living this way."

Sebastian watched him for a moment, then turned away, heading off at a good clip. "Maybe so. But living is better than dying, any day."

James snorted as the boy rounded the corner and was out of sight. "Shows what you know," he growled.

It didn't take much longer before he finished up. Once it was lit, the fire spread quickly and he left the building, locking the door behind him and pulling the hood of his cloak over his face. The sun was peeking over the horizon and he felt its oppressive heat even more than the fire that licked up the inside of the building.

Soon he could hear the screaming and he turned away, seeking the safety of shadow.

He couldn't wait to get out of this damn corset.

Grim Haunting

James Grim became sure that he was being followed as he passed through Budapest.

His awareness of it started far earlier than that, almost as soon as he crossed the French border into Germany, but the vague, subconscious suspicion didn't crystallize into certainty until he was almost out of Hungry and headed further east into the wild territory that had once been called Romania.

He had to admit, he was curious how long his unseen tail would stay on him, but so far he hadn't been able to shake him.

Or her.

Or it.

And that was the most confounding part - it always seemed like a different person, or no one at all. Whenever he was sure he could feel the observer's eyes upon him, he would turn and see yet another stranger suddenly averting their gaze or turning to cross the street.

One morning, he lay awake for an hour, considering the problem. He couldn't help but think of the young man he freed from the vampire nest in Marseilles. Of course, that boy was a vampire by now, so even if he were inclined to follow James - which he doubted - he had other concerns, like learning how to satisfy his bloodthirst without killing anyone.

Could it possibly be another shape shifter? But they were so rare; James doubted that he'd ever see another one.

No, the only explanation was that he'd picked up a group of people that were keeping tabs on him. Perhaps they were all part of an organization that was handing him off like some weird kind of relay race as he moved across Europe.

The tail kept up with him as he put down a group of uppity zombies in Prague, and a young hunger-crazed vampire in Budapest. But they didn't reveal themselves, or approach him, as the weeks passed.

The settled and civilized parts of Europe slowly fell away behind the wheels of his motorcycle. Walled cities and planted fields gradually gave way to desolation. All around him were patches of dense forest and crumbling buildings slowly being overcome by vines and mosses.

Despite how creepy the surveillance was, James forcibly put it out of his mind as he drove a winding path between the cracks of the damaged road. It was once a main thoroughfare through Romania towards Transylvania before the country fell to anarchy from a rather overwhelming excess of vampires and an unhealthy zombie infestation, and now the concrete was all humps and valleys and crazy zigzagged cracks that could easily turn a wheel.

Not only that, but from the sky poured torrential rains, accompanied by a kaleidoscope of lightening flashes. It was hard enough to keep his motorcycle on the busted-up road without obsessing over something he couldn't change. These people, whoever they were, would tell him what they wanted eventually, or give up and leave him alone. Either way, he'd be satisfied sooner or later. And meanwhile, he'd far rather obsess over the cold rain trickling down his spine and the wind blasting cold slaps of moisture across his face.

His intense musings on the subject of how he was definitely not going to think about the people following him anymore were interrupted by a loud bang as his motorcycle bucked underneath him. He slammed on the brakes and wrestled the bike for an instant before it flipped and he threw himself off of it. He tumbled across the muddy ground as the motorcycle slid in the other direction on the road, throwing up sparks that paled in comparison to the storm's fireworks above.

Finally James came to a stop, lying spread-eagled on the ground with the rain falling in his eyes.

"Well, fuck."

After a moment, he climbed painfully to his feet, shrugged his shoulders to settle his coat around him again, and moved to inspect the damage.

The shredded tire was obvious before he'd even reached his bike. Probably some junk left on the road had just gotten lucky and buried itself in his tire, resulting in the rather spectacular blowout. If he'd been human, especially considering he didn't bother with a helmet, he'd certainly have been killed.

Sometimes there were advantages in being a

vampire. Especially when they included really insanely fast reflexes.

There was other damage, but it looked mostly superficial. He righted the bike and started walking it, limping painfully. He was pretty sure he'd busted his leg in the fall, but it would heal.

Several hours later, he saw a lighted window and headed for it without hesitation. He couldn't imagine what sort of person still lived out here in this godforsaken land, but he couldn't exactly walk all the way to Transylvania, dragging his busted bike and nursing a sore ankle. The bone had knitted, but it still hurt like a bitch, and he was tired of walking in the rain.

Maybe they'd be friendly.

Yeah right.

When Grim reached the house, he barely spared its gothic gargoyles and looming trees a second glance. The place was huge, but he wouldn't have cared if it were a shack. It had a roof, and looked to be in good repair. It would surely be warm and dry inside.

He banged on the door, and waited for the ten seconds he deemed it polite before grabbing the knob and pulling it open with a rusty creak that stabbed into his brain like a silver ice pick.

"Hello?" he shouted into the darkness beyond the heavy door.

When he received no answer, he shrugged and wrestled his bike over the stoop. "My name's James Grim. I'm just going to invite myself in out of the rain, okay?"

He happily interpreted the silence to mean it was

okay.

"All right, then," he grumbled, leaning his bike against the nearest wall and going in search of a lantern and some matches that weren't soaking wet. The door closed with a groan and a boom, sealing out the weather.

* * *

With no parts to repair his bike, and a thunderstorm raging outside anyway, James didn't have much to do, so he spent the next little while exploring. He did find two lamps in the entranceway with oil still in the well and he lit them, leaving one on its hook and using the glow of the other one's flame to explore. He could get along in a pinch without light if he had to, but it was easier to keep from barking his shins on any low furniture if he had it.

Everything from the floors to the furniture were coated in a thin layer of dust, and the house smelled of moths, rats, and a powerful musty floral scent, but obviously hadn't been abandoned too long. There were no broken windows and there was no sign of rot.

He found the source of the light he'd seen in an upstairs bedroom window - another lamp, the oil almost gone and the flame guttering faintly. It, and the surface of the bureau immediately surrounding it were the only things not coated in dust, but they didn't look wiped clean, merely used frequently enough that dust never accumulated. The glass was extremely hot to the touch and it had to have been lit hours ago. He frowned at it as if it offended him.

Maybe whoever it was went out in the storm and left the light on to direct him home, he mused, and thoughtfully added more oil to it from a canister sitting on a shelf nearby. Just in case.

It sounded more plausible than any other idea, but in his entire search of the place, he'd seen no evidence of a person who might have lit the lamp. There wasn't so much as a footprint in the dust save his own. The bedroom was carpeted, but there were no prints on the wooden floor in the hall outside, either.

Who had lit the lamp, and where had they gone afterwards? Had they flown in and out the window like some kind of bird? So far as James knew, despite the legends, vampires couldn't fly.

Just as he left the bedroom, he heard the front doors open with another tooth-grinding shriek. A gust of wind blew into the house and danced around James' coat and hair, stirring the dust up into a fine, nose-itching cloud. James moved swiftly to the top of the wide staircase leading from the lobby to the second floor, a perfect vantage point to see the nature of his returning host.

But whoever it was didn't seem to belong there. Heavily wrapped in a long coat, hood up and pulled low against the rain, it looked more like some kind of wraith than a person. The intruder darted his head side to side, looking around furtively, then he or she closed the door and hesitated, as if trying to decide what to do next.

When it moved towards his precious motorcycle, James decided it was time to intervene.

"You there!" he shouted, running down the staircase on swift feet with his coat flaring out behind him. "Who are you?"

The figure froze like a deer in headlights, head jerking up to look at Grim. James caught a glimpse of a pale face and wide stormy eyes, and then the boy bolted.

Feet slipping on the smooth tile, the newcomer fled away from the motorcycle, into a dark room off to one side of the lobby that James knew from his earlier explorations was a sitting room.

The vampire darted after his prey, bloodlust slamming into him unexpectedly at the realization that the boy was fleeing from him in fear.

James had lit a lamp or two in the lobby before starting his explorations, but the room the boy had run into was pitch black. There wasn't even any light filtering in from outside, due to the heavy rain clouds. Almost as soon as the running figure entered the room there was a yelp and a crash as he tripped over an errant piece of furniture and fell headlong on the floor.

Grim was on him in an instant, discarding the lamp he carried carelessly as he pinned the struggling body. The lamp rolled across the floor, flame flickering wildly, and fetched up on the hearth.

Grim bared his teeth with a hiss and pulled the cowl from the boy's face, baring bright blond hair and a sweet, unblemished neck.

"No wait!" his prey screamed. "Please James, wait!"

His pulse beat visibly in his throat; a trapped butterfly Grim would free in a moment.

Grim bent to taste him, but paused, teeth dimpling that smooth skin.

He knew his name.

Why did he call him by name?

Bloodlust pulsed in James' brain like a diseased heart, but he raised his head with an effort, looking down into those terrified grey eyes. He'd seen that exact flavour of fear before.

"Sebastian?"

Relief flooded into Sebastian's face and he nodded hastily. "Yes, it's me. I-I'm sorry, I won't touch your bike. Will you please let me up?"

There was a moment when neither of them moved, and then James reluctantly drew back and rose to his feet. He bent to retrieve the lamp, which had thankfully neither broken nor lit the entire place on fire. Sebastian climbed to his feet as well, rubbing his elbow with a pained look on his face.

A few things were starting to add up now. "What the shit are you doing here, boy?" James demanded, turning on Sebastian with a frown. "Don't tell me you're the one who's been following me!" As a shapeshifter, Sebastian could have disguised himself as a hundred different people along the way. It really *had* been him.

He'd have thought of it sooner, except he'd been sure the kid was too smart to do something so idiotic.

A blush flooded Sebastian's cheeks. "Yeah," he said. "I've been kinda following you."

"Didn't I tell you if I saw you again I'd kill you?" James demanded. There was another thought in his mind attempting to connect itself with something else, but he pushed it away, far too angry to deal with it at the moment.

Sebastian shifted from foot to foot. "Technically

you said if you ever caught me preying on the innocent, you'd kill me," he said.

"And haven't you?" James demanded. There was no way a newly-reborn vampire could resist the call of his lust. No *way* in hell.

Sebastian shook his head quickly, taking an eager, and almost desperate, step towards him. "No! No, James, I haven't. I'm not a vampire - it didn't happen!"

"What?"

But James suddenly caught up with that niggling thought and realized he already knew. He would have smelled it in Sebastian's blood if he'd been a vampire. James would never have reacted the way he had - never have attacked another vampire for food.

"How is that possible?" he whispered, rocked to the core. "She bled you out, and you tasted her, didn't you?"

Sebastian shivered visibly, drawing his coat - which James saw was threadbare and looked scavenged from a dumpster somewhere - more closely around himself. His shoes were nearly worn off his feet, too. "She did," he said. "But I waited and waited, and I never turned into a vampire. I never got sick, and I never changed."

James searched his expression, but he already knew he wouldn't see a lie there. The evidence was right there in front of him.

"Maybe because you're a shapeshifter," he mused, frowning deeply. "You must be immune."

The boy nodded. "That's what I figured, too."

Grey eyes flicked away for a moment, then met James' again. "That's why I started following you."

"Meaning what? Why follow me?"

Sebastian sighed, and then sat down on a sofa, tucking his muddy feet up underneath him with no regard for the dusty, but fine upholstery. "Well," he said. "It's just that..."

James glanced at him when he trailed off, and saw something he hadn't wanted to truly notice - a shivering, forlorn figure wrapped up in a dirty coat way too big with him and full of holes besides.

He sighed. When had he gotten so damn soft?

"Come on," he heard himself say. "I think there are hot water facilities here, if they're still working. You should get warmed up before you shiver yourself to pieces."

What did it matter why the kid was following him? Really? He'd get around to telling him sooner or later.

Sebastian's head jerked up in surprise and a brilliant smile lit up his features. "Yeah, that sounds great."

James grunted. "I'll show you where they are."

* * *

Sebastian followed James up the stairs, hoping fervently that there really was hot water. His feet were sore, and he couldn't walk without limping as his cuts and blisters complained. His elbow was throbbing, too - it had taken most of the impact when he tripped over the ottoman in the other room.

But mostly he was wet, and *chilled*. He'd managed to catch rides most of the time that he was travelling, following James across Europe. It hadn't been that hard to keep up with him - living on the streets for most of his childhood, Sebastian had learned how to adapt.

A new vampire in town always caused talk, and when that vampire was supposedly called in by the city to help with some other problem, there was even more speculation and gossip. It didn't take Sebastian long to learn what rumours to follow, and there were usually those willing to give rides to certain faces. Beautiful women were dangerous to mimic, but people nearly always stopped for young girls and old grandmothers.

But when James had passed into the wilder realms, it had become harder and harder. Sebastian had stolen a car and wrestled it as far as he could, ignoring it when a tire blew out and bumping along slowly over the damaged road. But when it simply sputtered and died, one of the arrows on the dashboard pointing firmly at the red "E", Sebastian hadn't known how to make it go any further.

He'd been walking for hours along the road by the time he found the lighted house. Lost, alone and wondering why he'd ever left civilization to follow a stupid impulse out into cursed land, when he saw the light, he could have cried.

The fact that he had actually managed to catch up to James was almost enough to make him cry for real, even if the vampire had attacked him. Again.

He was in a fog at this point, too exhausted to really pay attention, so he nearly ran straight into the taller man when they reached the bathroom.

James looked at him askance, then gestured. "Here. All yours, I guess. No one seems to be here to tell us otherwise, anyway."

The room looked like a palace.

Tiled in white on the floor, wall and countertops, the bathroom would have gleamed had it not been covered by a thin layer of dust and grime. There was a sink with knobs that hadn't rusted much yet, a real water closet, and a claw-foot bathtub that was easily large enough for Sebastian to submerge himself.

The boy stepped forward and ran a finger through the dust coating the edge of the bathtub, then touched one of the silver-plated knobs next to the faucet. "What is this place, anyway?" he asked, turning to James.

The vampire paused, half-turned as he'd been about to leave. Somehow Sebastian didn't want him to go, though he knew no one sane would go back out into that storm without a good reason, vampire or not. James would only be elsewhere in the house; he couldn't get far.

"I have no idea," James said, glancing at him over his shoulder. "It's just a place we both found, and there doesn't seem to be anyone here. You okay with that thing?" he added, gesturing to the faucet. Sebastian was still touching it with the tips of his fingers, but hadn't tried messing with it, yet.

Sebastian blushed and glanced down at the knob. "I...think so. I turn this, right?" At James' nod, he grasped it and twisted and a cascade of water began flooding into the tub. He jumped, his eyes widening. He'd only seen running water a few times in his life - always from afar.

"That's it," James said, his lips crooking. "Make sure you use both, one should be hot and one cold. Test the water to make sure it's a good temperature before you put the stopper in and let it fill. Could get burned if you're not careful."

Sebastian nodded and smiled up at the vampire as he tested the two knobs. The water warmed quickly and steam rose into the air. "Thank you," he said. "I'll be okay."

The vampire left the room without another word, leaving his lantern on a hook and closing the door behind him. Alone in the dimly-lit and strange room, it took Sebastian a few minutes to work up the courage to undress and get into the steaming, slightly pungent water.

Once he was in, though, it was glorious.

The shivering stopped almost immediately. There was a small bar of real soap on the side of the tub. It was hard, but once he'd washed it off a few times in the stream from the faucet it started to soften up. He scrubbed himself until he was pink, allowing the greying water to run out of the drain and then filling the tub a second time before settling in to luxuriate in the sensations.

He laid there, head back and body supported by the water, for so long the water began to cool and his fingertips wrinkled. The only illumination in the room came from the lamp that James had left him, and the wavering light of the flame wasn't enough to brighten more than a small area of the room. He found he was falling asleep despite himself, sinking deeper and deeper into the water.

He dreamed there was a horrible, blood-curdling scream from somewhere nearby. The dream actually woke him and he jerked up into a sitting position, the cold water splashing and slopping out of the tub.

As he sat up, he thought he saw a girl in a faded print dress, standing just a few feet away. He started in surprise, a cry on his lips, but in a blink she was gone.

Heart racing, he looked around wildly, but there was no sign of the girl. He had to have dreamed her from the beginning.

His heart was just beginning to slow when the door slammed open with such force that it was nearly ripped from its hinges. "Kid!" James exclaimed as he burst through the doorway. "What's wrong?"

"Nothing!" Sebastian gasped, his heart racing all over again. "Nothing's wrong!"

"It wasn't you screaming?" James demanded, beginning to relax from his agitated posture as his expression flickered into irritated confusion. Sebastian saw a gun in his other hand, which James was holding low as if he didn't want it to be noticed.

It was huge for a pistol, with a long double barrel. It looked like it'd be too heavy for Sebastian to lift, let alone use.

Sebastian wrenched his eyes away from the weapon and up to James' face. *It wasn't a dream?* he thought. "It wasn't me," he croaked, his throat suddenly gone dry. The last of the heat had long drained out of the water and he realized he was shivering again. "I thought I heard a scream and it woke me up, and then I thought I saw someone, but then I really *must* have woken up for real. There was nothing there." He pointed to the spot where the girl had been standing.

James' lips thinned. "I've searched this house for hours. High and low. There isn't a single footprint in the dust that we didn't leave ourselves, and the only evidence that anyone lives here is that one lamp in the window."

There was a door standing slightly ajar close by to where the girl had been standing in Sebastian's dream. The inch-wide gap wasn't nearly wide enough for a person to fit through, and James had to pull it open to look inside. "This is just a closet, and there's no one in there," he said.

Sebastian shivered again and that time it wasn't from the cold. "Then who screamed?" he asked softly.

James only shook his head.

Silence stretched out for a few long minutes. Sebastian sat, shaking and straining his ears to try to hear something, anything, other than the blood rushing in his veins and his own breaths. But he heard nothing but the rain on the windows and the howl of the wind outside. No repetition of the scream, certainly. No other signs of life other than themselves.

Finally he stirred himself. "James?" he whispered, and the vampire started. Sebastian thought he had probably been listening, too. "Can I have a towel?" the boy asked apologetically.

James looked at him as if suddenly remembering he was there. "Oh," he said. "Let me find you one."

He turned and went into the closet, emerging quickly with a threadbare but large towel in his hand. "I found some clothes that might fit you while you were bathing," he said, holding the towel out.

Sebastian took it and covered himself as he stood, feeling oddly modest even though he knew James had seen him under far worse circumstances before. He remembered the feel of James' cock under his hand

and shivered at the memory.

Rubbing himself down, he watched the water drain out of the tub, afraid to look at James. He wondered if the vampire was watching him, maybe thinking about how good his blood had tasted.

No. He's not like that.

But it wasn't until he was completely dry and had the towel wrapped tightly around himself that he dared to look up. James wasn't looking at him at all, but was examining an old, faded bowl of coloured leaves.

"What is it?" Sebastian asked quietly, and James turned to look at him.

"Nothing," the older man said, shaking his head. "This potpourri stuff is everywhere in this house. It smells rank."

Sebastian frowned uncertainly. "Is it bad?" he asked. He could only smell a faint perfume, but he had noticed that it lingered in every room he'd been in so far.

James shrugged. "Just numbs the nose after a while," he said. "They use it in hospitals in some countries, because it covers the smell of sick people. I find it foul." He shook his head and headed for the door. "Come on. You're asleep on your feet." Sebastian moved to follow, padding barefoot out into the hallway.

"Thanks, James, for taking care of me like this," he offered with a smile.

James snorted. "Who's taking care of you?" he growled. "Just got nothing better to do, and I want to keep track of you, that's all. What with the screaming."

"Oh," Sebastian said, frowning down at his feet. But still he felt he was right about what was really under that gruff exterior. Despite everything, he felt reassured when James was around. He believed that James was different from other vampires, and that belief had carried him all the way from France.

But he could still only hope that his faith in the vampire wasn't misplaced.

* * *

Sebastian looked to be so exhausted he was swaying on his feet as they walked into the small bedroom where James had found the lamp, so James grabbed one of the sets of sleeping clothes he'd found and shoved them into Sebastian's arms. "Get dressed," he ordered, and the kid obediently dropped his towel.

James hadn't found any food in the kitchen, which was the most disused room in the house. "Don't suppose you brought any food along with you?" he asked tersely, turning away to poke through the closet, which was filled with little girls' dresses, many of which had suffered from the deprecations of moths.

He didn't expect a small hand to slip into his own, warm even though the leather of his gloves.

He glanced at the boy, seeing how his face jutted out pale and peaky over the light blue flannel of the pyjamas. With the grey eyes and blond hair, he looked like a ghost himself.

He was hung with the compelling aroma of fear, probably left over from the fright a few minutes before.

"Will you...stay for a bit?" Sebastian whispered, his gaze falling away. Blood chased itself across his cheeks, driving back some of the pallor. "I know you need to find somewhere dark to sleep before dawn, but...please?"

James turned his eyes heavenwards, sighing. If he'd been a praying man, he'd have been asking God for the forbearance to deal with stupid kids who wanted to snuggle up to vampires to chase away the ghosts. If James were in Sebastian's position, he'd have rather played with the evil spirits.

"Yeah," he heard himself say. "Sure. Whatever."

He didn't see the relieved smile spread across Sebastian's face, but he heard it in his voice. "Thank you, James. This place is just so... creepy."

James nodded, wondering why he was putting up with this. "I guess it's creepy, at that," he said, gently but firmly removing his hand from Sebastian's grasp. "But there's nothing here that can hurt you, so long as I'm around. Got it?"

"Got it," Sebastian said, and dear Lord, the kid actually sounded reassured.

Sebastian moved to the bed, which was at least sizeable, and James shrugged off his coat and stepped out of his boots. The gun harness went next, both of his girls clanking against the wood as he laid it on a chair.

He hadn't been able to bring his precious paired pistols along on his last major vampire hunt - lord knew, there just wasn't anywhere in a corset to keep a pistol whose barrel was half the length of your arm. From the shocked look in Sebastian's eyes earlier, he hadn't seen them before, even while stalking James for the last few months.

When Grim had first begun working for the Vatican, they'd outfitted him, and these guns were the most deadly weapons he could come up with. Thankfully the Vatican had agreed to have them made for him. Silver-plated, they were deadly to vampires even if all he did was pistol-whip them. Even better, if he fired the guns, the silver hollow point bullets contained holy water.

His biggest fear was that one day he'd come up against someone who was smart enough - and talented enough - to get them away from him.

He walked over to the bed and sat down next to Sebastian, who had gotten under the covers. The boy was sitting up, watching James' every move. "How do you want to do this?" James grunted.

And why did he have to look so damn small and vulnerable like that? It was worse than when he'd been a girl! On the other hand, James had to admit he liked him better this way, though he couldn't put his finger on exactly why.

Sebastian shrugged and the collar of the pyjamas fell slightly askew, baring one shoulder. "Uh, are you really asking me?" he asked. There was a chain around his neck and James remembered the silver cross.

"Sure I'm asking you," James said, rolling his eyes. "You asked me to stay, so spit it out. Where do you want me?"

Sebastian was amusing when he squirmed, but he seemed to know just where he wanted James - leaned up against the headboard, with Sebastian curled up against his chest and practically in his lap. James allowed himself to be manipulated by Sebastian's hands with a sense of bemusement.

Finally they were settled and Sebastian was out like a light thirty seconds later. James was left to stare into the dimness and brood.

There were a few things to mull over, foremost of which was the warm, vibrant young man snuggled up against him. What the hell was he going to do with him? Abandoning him in the house was vaguely tempting. At least he'd have shelter, if no food, but if James was honest with himself he knew he couldn't take that step.

Sebastian was vampire bait, and given where they were, if a vampire didn't already live here, one would soon move in.

Even taking that into account, there was the question of the motorcycle. The last source of parts was some miles behind him and heaven knew there was unlikely to be anything ahead other than more desolation. Sebastian would never be able to keep up with him on foot, either. No human could match James' endurance and speed over the long haul, even burdened with the machine.

There was nothing for it. He had to go back.

And he had been looking forward to a good bit of hunting in the wastes, too. Damnit.

Just as he came to this disheartening conclusion, another shriek echoed through the house.

Sebastian jerked awake at the sound and his arm came up, wrapping around James' neck and clinging tightly as the scream went on and on.

"What can it be? No! No don't leave me!" Sebastian exclaimed, the latter part because James had been trying to extricate himself from his grasp and go investigate the source of the sound.

To his vampire ears, it sounded like it was coming from all around them. It had a male timbre and was definitely inside the house, but he could hear it coming from somewhere in the room, and further down the hallway, and even downstairs. How was that possible?

He stood, pulling Sebastian forcibly off of him, but by the time his feet hit the floor, the scream had already cut off as if by a knife. He stood, ears cocked, Sebastian's hand curled tightly in the tail of his shirt, but again there was nothing more to hear.

He glanced down at the boy. Sebastian was trembling, holding James' shirt so tightly the vampire didn't think he could free himself without ripping the fabric.

"Sorry...I'm sorry," Sebastian said after a moment, uncurling his hand reluctantly.

Sighing, James dropped down heavily onto the bed. "I don't know what's going on," he said. "But it's a little bit important to find out, don't you think?"

Sebastian wasn't looking at him. His teeth were just visible, chewing on his lower lip. James scented a tiny bit of blood and reached for him automatically. Sebastian curled gratefully into his arms. "I guess," the boy said reluctantly. "I just think this place is haunted. Why else would I have seen a ghost before? Why else would there be no footprints?"

"I've never met a real ghost," James admitted. He pulled off his gloves and set them on the bedside table, shifting to resume their former position. His fingers combed lightly through Sebastian's hair in an absent motion. "I thought they were a bloody crock, though after this...I might have to change my mind."

Sebastian nodded, relaxing against him. "Sorry I stopped you," he said softly. "I was just scared. This place..."

James leaned his head back against the wall. Hunger curled in his stomach, awakened by that tiny spot of blood on Sebastian's lower lip. It wasn't even visible, but he could smell it, and he hadn't had a good meal in a long while. The injury from earlier had depleted his stores even further.

"I'm the one who should scare you," he muttered. "Why did you follow me here, kid? Why follow me at all? You were free of the virus. Why didn't you just go on with your life?"

"I..." Sebastian curled up a little further, his arm tightening around James' waist. "I didn't want to go on with my life."

He looked up, something old and jaded in his grey eyes. His mouth was pulled down in a solemn frown. "My life sucks, James. In case you hadn't noticed."

"Sucks?" James echoed, raising an eyebrow. "What makes you think I know enough about you to even guess that?" *And what does that have to do with anything, anyway?*

Sebastian shrugged. "I dunno, I just thought you were pretty smart."

James reacted to that before he thought. "I am smart," he exclaimed, sitting up a little further. "Where do you get off saying that, brat?"

Then he realized that Sebastian was grinning, and settled against the wall, grumbling. "Tell me why your life 'sucks'," he demanded in a growl. He wasn't going to let Sebastian get away with trying to change the subject.

Sagging, Sebastian glanced away again and settled his head against James' shoulder. In that position, James had a beautiful, tempting view of the back of his neck, and the vampire deliberately chose to study the ceiling.

"I don't have a home to go to, James," he said. "I've lived on the street most of my life. You say I should have gone on with my life, but what life did I have? Living in an alley stealing food to survive? That's no life."

James was quiet for a moment, realizing belatedly that he *should* have realized that. Sebastian had mentioned that he lived on the streets when they'd last met, but James had forgotten, or perhaps he hadn't been listening.

"Yeah," James said with a sigh. "That's no life at all."

He glanced down, grasping Sebastian by the chin and forcing him to sit up enough to meet his eyes. "But that doesn't explain why you've been following me. Out with it."

Sebastian blushed again and tried to draw back, to pull his chin from James' grasp, but James held him still and he was forced to look steadily into his eyes as he spoke. "I...I wanted to be like you," he admitted, the blush creeping down his neck and out to the tips of his ears. "I wanted to learn to be strong, to fight vampires and zombies, so I can have a life like yours, and not have to be afraid of them anymore."

What?

James felt the slack look of shock and amazement

on his own face, as the surprise hit him like a fist to the gut. "Are you *insane*?" he demanded. "You want to be like *me*?"

There was something shining in Sebastian's eyes, and it wasn't tears.

It was...hero worship. Oh god.

The kid nodded quickly. "You never have to be afraid of anything. You have all of the food you could ever want, and stay in the nicest inns, and never want for anything. You just go wherever you please, and you help people, and you're so strong that nothing can hurt you."

"I don't need food, nor soft beds," James reminded him with a growl. Sure he stayed in inns when he travelled - but he shut himself in during the *day*. And when the sleep of day had him in its thrall, he could be sleeping on a bed of nails and he'd never notice.

And Sebastian was missing the most important factor. "And I'm a *vampire*."

Doubt flickered in Sebastian's eyes. "Well...I know," he said. "And I don't want that. But there are humans who hunt vampires, and I'm better than human. I can do a lot of things that normal people can't do, and I'm sure I'd make a good hunter, if I just had a little training."

Shimmering, hopeful grey eyes turned upwards to James. "I hoped you would help me. I can be your part-- your sidekick. See? I'll be like an apprentice."

James gave his well-considered decision without a moment's hesitation.

"Forget it."

Sebastian's face fell, but he looked up a moment later, his expression set with determination. "You say that now," he said. "But I'll show you I can be useful!"

Annoyance flickered through James, and his eyes narrowed. "Not only are you a fool for even asking for this," he snapped. "But you're worse than useless, kid. You're soft, and untrained. I work alone, and you'll only drag me down."

"That's not true!" Sebastian exclaimed, to James' surprise. He'd been expecting sagging defeat, not this. Then again, Sebastian had followed him this far. He did have a bit of fire in him, at that.

Not that James would tell him so in a thousand years. It would only encourage this stupidity.

"It *is* true," he said implacably. "Look at you - you're so afraid of some stupid ghost stories you can't even sleep alone."

A flush spread across Sebastian's cheeks and he shoved hard at James' shoulders, pushing himself up to sit more than moving the vampire. "Shut up!" he exclaimed. "I'm not soft, and I'm not a scaredy cat. I could do just fine without you - I just don't want to! And I'll show you I'm brave, and help you at the same time."

"Oh, and just what are you--"

Something glinted in Sebastian's hand as he raised it and James suddenly realized that he had one of the knives he kept strapped to his thigh. The little scamp had nicked one of the silver knives without him ever realizing it. When had he taken it?

"You attacked me before," Sebastian said, and James stiffened, wondering if the kid was planning on stabbing him with his own goddamned knife. "You're hungry, aren't you?"

And before James could react, the boy brought the knife down in a slashing motion, opening up a vein in his own wrist.

He didn't look as though he'd expected it to hurt so much. Sebastian's mouth opened in an 'O' of startled shock and pain and his eyes watered up, but he shoved the bleeding wound towards James and the rich, hot scent of his blood filled his nostrils. The vampire surged forward, grabbing the boy's hand and bringing it to his mouth.

And once again that beautiful *sparkle* ran over his lips and down his throat.

"Y-you see," Sebastian gasped, slumping against him and tossing the knife aside to clatter on the floor. "I'm not afraid."

Grim scarcely heard him, shifting to push the boy down onto the bed. Somewhere in the back of his mind he remembered the last time he had tasted him, and his hand began to wander, stroking over the flannel that covered Sebastian's stomach and then down his thigh. His own cock began to swell and he rubbed against Sebastian's thigh, awakening his own arousal further.

The whimper his prey gave only spurred him on, especially when a small, questing hand slid between them and began to rub at his erection through his pants.

He tugged the pyjamas down, vaguely remembering that Sebastian had stopped him the last time. But this time the boy allowed it, gasping and rocking up as he curled his fingers around his member and it awakened in his hand.

"J-James," Sebastian moaned as Grim stroked him

gently, up and down, and his cock lengthened in James' hand.

The blood still flooded into the vampire's mouth, but it was a vague trickle compared to the rich, pulsing veins in Sebastian's throat. But there was another artery, deeper, just beyond his reach and he bit down hard, fangs seeking the rich, oxygenated blood that was too deep for the knife to reach.

Sebastian let out a scream and his hand stopped rubbing at James' groin as his whole body began to tremble. "Please stop!" Sebastian pulled his hand up and pushed at James' shoulder. "That hurts!"

Perhaps it was the slower trickle of blood compared to the last time, but James was able to gather the shreds of his mind together at Sebastian's plea. He licked at the wound one last time, savouring the flavour, and lifted his head, turning his eyes to meet the boy's.

"I thought you weren't afraid," James rasped. His hand was still moving automatically over Sebastian's cock, which had softened somewhat.

"It still *hurts*," Sebastian hissed angrily, and James found himself smiling. He did have spirit.

"That it does. And you're nicely accommodating, despite it," he said. The faint thread of gratitude running through his words wasn't feigned. For all that Sebastian had obviously had something to prove, James knew he had also done it out of a twisted desire to be helpful.

The words brought a faint, pained smile to Sebastian's face and James gave into an impulse. He bent his head to kiss him.

That produced a combination of sounds that were

a bit difficult to untangle. There was definitely a grunt of disgust as he tasted the blood on James' lips. But there was also an undercurrent of deep, heartfelt pleasure and Sebastian pressed upwards a moment later, returning the kiss.

James purred, his fangs nicking the boy's lips and producing just a bit of that delicious sparkle for him to feed upon as he rewarded Sebastian for his generosity. A give-and-take relationship like this wasn't exactly something he had tried before, but as Sebastian tugged his belt open and slipped his hand inside to stroke his cock with hard, rapid pulls, James realized that there might be something to it, after all.

They rocked together for a long while, tongues tangling, hands stroking one another harder and faster. Sebastian soon was jerking roughly in James' hands, orgasm sending fluid flooding over James' hand.

"Good," James soothed him automatically as Sebastian dropped back against the pillow, his hand faltering in its rhythm. He beamed lopsidedly and blinked his eyes sleepily open to smile up at him.

The warmth James felt at that smile had everything to do with his own impending climax, and that was it. Or so he told himself as he came shuddering over the fine fabric of Sebastian's pyjamas.

As the pulses of pleasure started to fade, James bent over Sebastian, licking lightly at the pulsepoint of his throat and enjoying the faint shudders and sighs it produced. Did Sebastian fear that he would bite him again? Perhaps. But the soft skin, with his faint aroma of rich redness was too tempting not to sample. Just a little. Even if he didn't actually bite.

Then just as James began to recover from the feeding frenzy and orgasm, Sebastian stiffened and let out a shriek.

James whipped around, just in time to see a flicker of movement at the window. He received just a faint impression of fluttering cloth and a pale, moon-shaped face, but before he had a chance to take it in, there was nothing but the waving shadows of the branches of the trees outside. "What? What was that?" he demanded, turning back to Sebastian and pushing himself up to sit.

Sebastian sat up with him, his arms tight around James' neck. "It was the ghost!" Sebastian exclaimed. "The girl. I saw her again - I *know* I did!"

James' lips thinned and he glanced back at the window. The wound on Sebastian's wrist was still smeared with blood, but was closing quickly due to the healing properties of his saliva. James' nostrils flared, but he felt only the smallest curl of hunger. The kid really had helped him, after all.

Carefully, he extricated himself from Sebastian's grasp. He'd seen *something*. He just wasn't sure what it was. "I'm going outside, to see if I can figure out what that thing is," he said. "Wait here," he added, turning a narrowed gaze on the boy. Sebastian was pale and sweating, even weaker than he had been before. Considering how spent he had been when he arrived, bleeding out for a vampire had not been smart.

To James' relief, Sebastian nodded, laying down and pulling the blankets up to his chin. "I'll stay here," he said in a soft, uncertain voice.

James nodded and rose from the bed. He threw his coat over his shoulders and pulled one of his guns from the holster, heading out the window in a whisper of leather.

He dropped down and landed in the overgrown garden below in a squelch of mud.

The rain closed over his head and within moments of going outside he was drenched again. The lightning had all but stopped and the darkness was oppressive, though his internal clock told him that it was close to dawn. You'd never know it from the sky, however. There wasn't even the faint indigo glow of pre-dawn - just iron grey clouds and endless rain.

As he moved away from the building, his eyes turning up towards the glowing window where Sebastian could be found, he caught sight of a white shape.

It skittered across the roof like a spider, climbing over the eaves and up towards the peak of the roof. It moved *fast* - from where James was standing, it looked as fast or faster than a vampire. And through the rain he could barely make it out, but it looked vaguely human shaped.

But no human could crawl so nimbly over the rooftop of that house without a misstep, and certainly not at that speed.

Then as he was watching, it went behind a point jutting up from the roof and vanished, not reappearing from the other side. James cursed and darted to his left, circling the building as quickly as he could, but he didn't catch another glimpse of the creature. Where had it gone?

When he reached the back of the house, where

several straggly trees and bushes surrounded a courtyard that must have once had a beautiful lawn, but was now overrun with weeds, he craned his neck to look up. He peered through the curtain of rain and faintly made out the shape of a window in the rooftop. There was an attic, and that window had to lead into it.

"Bloody hell," he muttered. "Do we have a nest of something up above us, then? Best get back to the boy before he gets himself into trouble again."

As he walked back around the house and went inside - through the front door this time - he frowned as he tried to work it out. Where the hell was the access to the attic? Surely there was a way in from the house, and he had just missed it. But he'd even looked in the closets, aware that most attics were accessed through trap doors in the ceiling, and there had been nothing.

He shook the worst of the rain out of his coat and squeezed out his hair on the grimy lobby floor as he headed for the stairs. A moment later, he walked into Sebastian's bedroom. "Well, I saw something. Looks like they're living up--"

He stumbled to a halt, staring at the disarranged and empty bed, and the gun harness on the chair.

Sebastian was gone, and so was his second pistol.

* * *

Almost as soon as James had left the house to investigate the ghost, the screaming had started up again. A series of short, sharp cries echoed through the house, and despite the way it made Sebastian shudder, he knew he had to investigate.

He had grabbed the second pistol, and the silver knife he had used to cut his own wrist, and gone looking for the source of the sound.

A minute later, the shrieking stopped, but not before Sebastian had made a significant discovery. When he heard James' distinct voice swearing up a storm, he emerged from the bedroom's closet. "James!" he exclaimed, and the vampire whirled around and started for him.

"Bloody hell, kid, where the fuck were you?" he demanded, grabbing Sebastian by the shoulders and giving him a little shake. His hair was plastered down by the rain and his blue eyes were wide.

Sebastian looked up at him, feeling a kernel of warmth grow in his chest. James had been worried. He grinned and pulled out of his grasp. "I'll show you. I think I know where the ghosts are."

"They're not ghosts," James said sharply. "I don't know *what* they are, but they're solid."

"I know," Sebastian said, opening the closet door wide and stepping back inside. He gestured up at a hole in the ceiling, where he had removed the grate. It wasn't a trap door, but a grille that led into the ventilation system. It was just big enough for him to wriggle through, and he already had investigated enough to know it led to a network of passages he suspected ran over the whole top floor of the house.

"That's how you get to the attic," he explained. "And there are grates all over the house. I bet there's one in that bathroom closet. Whoever that girl is, that's how she's getting in and out."

He glanced back at James, who was nodding.

"Makes sense," he said. "Old ventilation shafts that they're using to get around. But *I* can't use it. Get back to bed, kid, I know another way in."

Sebastian lifted his chin stubbornly, and stepped up onto the shelf below the grate. From there, he knew he could pull himself up. "I'm going this way. I'll meet you there."

"Hell no," James said sternly. "You're staying here."

"I am not!" Sebastian argued. Frustration made him reach up and boost himself through the hole. He had thought James might act this way, but he'd just have to show him. He could handle this.

"Hey!" James exclaimed, and Sebastian felt a hand close around his foot, pulling back with incredible strength.

He yelped and kicked out. "Stop it! I'm going!" Twisting around himself like a snake, he bashed James' hand with the muzzle of the heavy pistol.

James exclaimed and jerked back, and Sebastian was suddenly free. Turning to face the passage again he crawled forward quickly, out of James' reach. Guilt squeezed his heart, but he moved forward determinedly on his elbows and knees, pistol in one hand and knife in the other. He had forgotten that the gun was silver-plated. Hopefully he hadn't hurt James too badly.

Though it was dark in the passage, and choked with dust, light filtered through the grates here and there, giving Sebastian enough to see by. He wasn't looking for a light from below, however, but a light from above.

It didn't take long to find.

Bright light shone down through a square hole in the ceiling, and Sebastian cautiously poked his head up through, looking around.

He seemed to be in an alcove or closet of some kind, and couldn't see anything at all except for a forest of metal legs and wheeled carts. A metallic clattering sound came from somewhere in the room, along with a low soft muttering that sounded like a male voice.

Sebastian climbed out of the hole as quietly as he could, aware that his pyjamas were coated in dust - not to mention his own blood - and wondering if he looked like a ghost as well. He crept forward noiselessly and peeked out of the alcove.

The room was spacious and well-lit both by electric bulbs and oil lamps situated all around. Two cots dominated the centre of the room, both occupied, and a tall, lanky figure in a white coat moved from one to the other. He looked like a doctor, and he was humming to himself as he worked. The stench of the potpourri was strong and Sebastian saw little baskets of it all over the place.

The figure in the bed closest to Sebastian was definitely dead. It was male - which was obvious, as it was uncovered and completely nude - but it completely lacked a head and its left leg ended at mid thigh. Both stumps looked surgical in nature, as if cut by a sharp knife. Tubes and wires extended from them and ran into bags and equipment. One of the bags suspended over the body was filled with blood, the others with less easily identifiable substances.

Sebastian recoiled slightly at the gruesome sight, swallowing bile, but forced himself to turn his attention to the other body.

If anything, that was even worse.

The second figure lacked both arms, and one leg, but it was definitely alive. The man didn't appear to be breathing, but he moved slightly, shifting against restraints that bound him securely to the bed.

The doctor was doing something at the lower part of his body, and suddenly spoke up more loudly. "Well, the tissue is cut through," he said in a jovial tone. "Time to deal with the bone, eh, Luiza?"

"Yes, doctor," came a second voice, and Sebastian's head whipped around to look in the direction it had come. The girl he had seen before was sitting on a countertop, stockinged legs swinging slightly, watching the proceedings. She looked to be perhaps six years old, small and pale in her frilly dress. She was soaked with water from head to toe, but didn't seem bothered by it.

She turned her head and met Sebastian's eyes, and the boy froze in shock. She'd seen him! And now Sebastian saw that fangs protruded from her lips.

A metallic squeal assaulted Sebastian's ears and both observers turned to watch the doctor once again. He lifted up the bone saw, whose round blade rotated so fast that Sebastian couldn't see the tines. Then he brought it down and the tenor of the sound changed.

He was cutting off the man's leg.

Sebastian watched the horror for a few seconds, rooted to the spot, and then the man on the table woke up and started screaming.

"Oh dear Lord in Heaven," Sebastian exclaimed, barely audible over the shrieking of the tortured man. The knife in Sebastian's hand clattered forgotten to the floor as he pulled the silver cross from his shirt and clutched it like a lifeline.

There was a hiss and suddenly the girl was standing right in front of Sebastian, her pointed teeth bared. He hadn't seen her move. "Put that away. Doctor, he's being a bad boy!"

The sound of the saw ceased and the doctor turned, ignoring the ongoing, but diminishing screams. The man was youthful, his face slender and pointed, spattered with fine drops of blood. He, too, was a vampire, and he glared at the cross in Sebastian's hand.

"Who are you?" he demanded. "Why are you interrupting my work?"

The doctor set down the saw and picked up a syringe. "Luiza, bring the boy here, my darling."

Luiza grabbed Sebastian by the wrist, avoiding the cross and taking hold of the arm he was holding the pistol with. Forgetting about the cross in his hand, Sebastian cried out and tried to pull away, but her grip was far too strong.

The doctor turned away from the struggle and brought the syringe down towards the neck of the man on the table. Before he could inject him, a few things happened in quick succession.

Sebastian brought the pistol up and fired blindly. The force of the discharge ripped him from Luiza's grasp and backwards to lie on the blood-soaked floor, stunned.

The bullet tore through Luiza's arm, leaving a smoking black hole, and buried itself in the doctor's stomach. The doctor shrieked and dropped his syringe, stumbling backwards against the table bearing the inert body, and clutching at the wound.

And James Grim crashed through the single window in the ceiling, dropping to the floor in a rain of glass shards. Suddenly the sound of the storm was quite close, rain pattering down onto him as a fork of lightning lit the sky.

"You! Both of you! Get out!" the doctor screamed, waving his free hand at Grim and crooking his fingers into claws. "Luiza!"

But Luiza wasn't listening. She gazed down at the blood soaking into her dress for a moment, and then took off like a spooked cat. She bounded up onto a table, dug her remaining hand into the wall and spidered up its sheer surface in a blur, and finally disappeared out into the rain.

Sebastian climbed to his feet, looking around at the destruction. The man on the table was no longer screaming, but his eyes were open and rolling in their sockets. Whimpers issued in a stream from his mouth. He, too was a vampire, and he had bitten through his own lips so many times that his chin was masked in dried blood.

The sounds made Sebastian feel that he might go mad.

James turned on the doctor and grabbed him by the collar, hauling him up to his feet. "What are you doing here?" the hunter snapped, his face inches from the other vampire. "Why are you torturing him?" He thrust out his other hand, pointing the pistol straight at the unfortunate vampire on the table.

"Torturing? No, no!" the doctor exclaimed. He didn't struggle, but turned his head to look at the man on the table with a sick fawning expression that turned Sebastian's stomach. "He is my love. My Eli. He's dying!"

"Dying?" James shoved the man away from him in disgust. "Of course he's dying! You're fucking cutting him to pieces!" He levelled the pistol at the doctor's forehead.

"No! You don't understand!" The doctor put his hands together in a pleading expression. "His body...it's diseased. I gave him the kiss of love centuries ago, but now there is something wrong with him. His face is still beautiful but his body is weakening by the year. No amount of blood can sustain him."

"That's impossible," Grim snarled. Sebastian was surprised to hear the depth of anger in James' voice. "Vampires don't get sick."

"I...I know," the doctor said. He reached out and put a hand on the body on the other table, stroking its strong and muscled chest and leaving a smear of blood behind. Now Sebastian was close enough to see that the body's three limbs had been stitched to the body with tiny, neat stitches.

"Dear God," he whispered, a true and honest prayer.

"Don't interrupt," Grim snapped, turning the force of his gaze on Sebastian for only an instant before returning his gaze to the doctor, who went on.

"I'm giving him a new body," the doctor whispered, his voice thick with anticipation and pride. "He'll still have the arms that he held me with, the legs that he walked with before he became too weak. Soon I'll find how to transfer his head without killing him, and then I will have my love back."

"Stupid fuck."

Sebastian was surprised to hear the words come out of his own mouth, but James had said the same thing, even louder, and no one paid Sebastian any mind. James continued. "You stupid *fuck*. You can't cut his head from his heart, or he'll ash. And after what you've done to him, he can't be sane!"

"His heart is diseased!" the doctor wailed. "I opened him up when he first began to fail, and there were lumps and lesions. If I don't give him a new heart, he'll surely die. I didn't want to hurt him, but the drugs I have...they aren't enough."

A soft, broken whisper reached Sebastian's ears and he turned towards the man on the table.

"Please..." the man whispered through his broken and bloody lips. He turned his head, fixing a beseeching gaze on Sebastian. "Please, let me go, my love."

Sebastian raised the pistol and fired.

The bullet punched straight into Eli's forehead and buried itself in the table. Sebastian was thrown back by the recoil against a table full of equipment and it overturned, crashing to the floor in a shower of sparks.

"NO!" the doctor screamed, but a second discharge from James' pistol silenced him. Before Sebastian had gained his feet again, the doctor had dropped like a stone and both vampires had begun to dissolve into ash.

Sebastian straightened, looking to James and realizing that he was beginning to shiver. He didn't feel cold, but he realized in an almost clinical way that the horrors he'd just seen had put him into shock.

"I killed him," he whispered, the gun falling from nerveless fingers to land with a thud on the floor. "I killed Eli. He asked me to."

James moved swiftly towards him, scooping up the pistol before pulling the boy tightly against him. Sebastian closed his eyes and melted into the protective circle of James' arms.

"You did just fine, kid," James whispered. "It was a mercy."

James tightened his arms. "It was a mercy to kill both, the mad bastards."

Sebastian nodded, burying his face into James' chest. He couldn't agree more.

A Grim Christmas Carol

Among dirty, smelly cities, Prague stood out as one of the dirtiest and smelliest. But tonight, as they bumped and jolted over the badly maintained roads in their slow quest towards a place to rest for the day, there was a strange, lightened atmosphere to the stench that James Grim couldn't quite identify.

Maybe it was the goddamned truck he was driving.

After leaving the 'haunted' house in the wilds of what used to be known as Russia, James and Sebastian had made their way back towards civilization in search of replacement parts for his beloved motorcycle. Thankfully they had found an old truck in the mansion's large garage, and were able to load James' motorcycle onto the flatbed.

The truck had seemed at first glance to be nothing but a lonely, rusted hulk, long ago wasted away to nothing in a room big enough for several vehicles. But when Grim had tried the key, it had started - reluctantly, but it started, and it had gotten them this far.

The truck was every bit the piece of crap it looked like, though. It belched blue and black smoke from the tailpipe and they had had to add oil to the engine every few hours along their way for fear the whole works would seize up. Even when the road was smooth, the truck rattled, shook and jolted along so violently that James wondered if it would simply shiver to pieces when it finally gave up and lost whatever stubborn spirit had held it together so long.

Of course, it also seemed to be made up of one solid piece of steel placed on top of a pair of axles and bald rubber tires, so perhaps when it was ready to give up the ghost it could have one last hurrah of usefulness as a battering ram. But for all that James had come to loathe and curse the truck for every bone-jarring kilometre of road, it had at least gotten them this far without actually dying on them.

That would be more satisfying if it weren't for the fact that James would have rather been almost anywhere but here. Unfortunately, Prague was where James had purchased his motorcycle, and therefore Prague was where he was most likely to find a way to fix it. Plus, it hadn't been out of his way.

Sebastian had no such qualms. He was, in fact, glued to the passenger side window and even more cheerful than the usual default level Grim had become accustomed to over the last few weeks of travelling together.

The reason for that became clear a moment later as Sebastian turned around and beamed at James, eyes shining like stars. "James," he said. "Do you see all the lights and things? It's *Christmas Eve*."

"What?" James stared at Sebastian for a moment,

then actually took a serious look around as they rattled to a stop in front of a hotel. The building itself was festooned with little twinkling lights - apparently this place was rich enough to afford the fuel for an electric generator, a good sign. There was also a pine wreath on the door.

He didn't normally pay that much attention, since holidays generally didn't include him. But now the snow that blanketed the sidewalks and road suddenly took on a different meaning, as James counted up the dates.

It *was* Christmas. No wonder something had seemed...off.

"So what?" he growled, killing the engine- possibly putting it out of its misery - and opening the door to get out of the cab.

Shockingly, Sebastian's bright expression didn't even falter. "So what? It's *Christmas*, James. You're a Christian, too. Don't you like Christmas?"

Twitch twitch twitch.

Then Sebastian dropped the biggest bombshell of them all.

"Jesus' *birthday* is tomorrow!"

The vampire flinched so hard he missed a step and banged his toe on the curb. His steel-toed boot rang like a bell and he stumbled up onto the sidewalk, colliding with a woman who was hurrying past. There were a few people out tonight, more than he would have expected. Perhaps leaving parties that had run late or busy enough to feel the need justified the risk of being outside at this hour. Obviously there wasn't a vampire in this area, or that would never happen.

Well, no vampires other than *him*.

But that wasn't what he was focussed on right at the moment. He reached out and grabbed Sebastian by the collar, yanking him closer and nearly pulling him right off his feet. "*Stop* that. Don't *say* that name. Now who says I'm a Christian anyway?" he hissed.

Sebastian swallowed visibly and for the first time his expression faltered. "Well you...you work for the Vatican, you know," he said softly. "I assumed, especially since you're a--"

Grim cleared his throat, loudly. "Shut up. You assumed wrong, kid," he growled. With a jerk, he let Sebastian go and the boy stumbled back a step, reaching up to rub his throat with an almost sheepish expression.

"Sorry James, I--"

"Excuse me."

James blinked. The quavering, female voice took him a moment to place, and then he turned to face the woman he had bumped into when he stumbled.

"What?" he asked.

The woman was dark skinned, wrinkled and stooped with age and holding a thick woollen shawl wrapped tightly around her head and shoulders.

She was glaring at him.

"You bump into a lady and don't apologize? You nearly knocked me off my feet! And then you treat your son like this? Shame on you, sir," she snapped.

My SON? Grim thought, choking. His mood was souring by the minute, and it was starting to seem like a conspiracy. He shook it off and glared back at the woman impatiently, though he kept his lips almost closed as he spoke, to hide his fangs. "What of it?"

Her dark eyes flashed. "Did your mother teach

you no manners?"

"James--"

"I'm *sorry* ma'am," Grim growled. "My mother was well-versed in manners, but apparently none of it transferred to me. Don't you have something to do other than bother me?"

"*James,*" Sebastian hissed, tugging on James' coat. "Please, let's just go inside. I'm very sorry, ma'am, he's..."

"Best idea I've heard all day," James said, turning away from the angry old lady and heading for the door to the hotel.

"And on Christmas Eve, too!" the woman huffed in disbelief. "Curse you!"

"Bah! Humbug," Grim snarled. The effect of his exit was somewhat spoiled when he hit the threshold and hovered there for a moment before Sebastian grabbed his hand and invited him into the building by the simple expedient of hauling him inside.

James reached back and slammed the door behind him with a satisfying crash.

* * *

The main floor of the inn was packed with people in the middle of a party. On some long trestle tables, the remains of a sumptuous dinner lay congealing. A group of people stood in one corner, playing carols on a mismatched variety of instruments.

There was a group of young girls near the door, and as James and Sebastian entered the building one of them tossed her shoes over her shoulder, nearly hitting the pair. James dodged the shoe and said nothing as the girls cheered and congratulated the girl for something. Apparently the way the shoes had fallen meant something good, but James couldn't imagine what.

"It's a Christmas party, James," Sebastian said excitedly. "Look at all those apples!" At one table, another group of people were cutting apples and exclaiming over the results. Who were these superstitious fools, anyway?

James grunted. "If you want to eat one, ask them," he said. "But this isn't our party. We just want a room."

His words didn't seem to dim Sebastian's enthusiasm, but the boy stuck close to his side as James tried to ignore the festivities all around them and track down the innkeeper to arrange for a room. It took only a few moments, and James was careful to keep his fangs hidden during the transaction. No sense in ruining it for everyone. Soon they were headed upstairs.

The room wasn't large, but it had a bed - fortunately free of bedbugs - a washing basin, and even a locking door. The best part, though - and you can bet this had cost James a pretty penny - was the fireplace.

Not only was there already a fire crackling in the hearth when they arrived, but there was a very comfortable looking easy chair set in front of said fire that practically had James' name on it. He sat down before he'd even shaken the snow off of his coat or taken his hat off.

Sebastian wandered about the room a moment. James had noticed that the boy had a way of doing that no matter where they went. The boy would explore every corner of a room, reaching out to touch anything that interested him, even picking it up and deliberately replacing it in such a way that no one would know it had been moved. He wondered if it was because the first place they'd stayed together had turned out to have hidden passages and insane vampires in it. But he suspected this behaviour long predated Sebastian's association with James.

And even now, there was still that spring in his step, an eagerness that James couldn't understand. So what if it was Christmas? What did that have to do with them? They had no families to share it with, no turkeys to eat or presents to give. Let the people have their bit of fun, sure, but leave James out of it.

Sebastian splashed a bit of water on his face, then rubbed it with the towel, yawning. For the most part, the shape-shifter had converted over to James' nighttime schedule in the weeks they'd been travelling, but James had noticed that he didn't sleep well. For all that Sebastian maintained that irrepressible optimism and happiness - even when it wasn't Christmas - the boy suffered from vicious nightmares. He tossed and turned, and from what few words he had cried out in his sleep, James was convinced that he was dreaming about vampires.

Whether it was the horrific medical scene they had recently witnessed, or the memories of being raped and bitten back in France, James didn't know. Perhaps both.

He didn't like to think that the face Sebastian saw in his dreams was Grim's own, but when he awoke during the day and listened to Sebastian crying out, the thought never failed to cross his mind regardless.

"Take the bed," James said. "It's pretty small. You can putter around during the day while I'm asleep and enjoy your Christmas if you want."

Lord help him, that was apparently the right thing to say. Sebastian's eyes lit up again and he beamed. "Really? Thank you, James!" he said, practically bouncing towards the bed. "I don't ever get presents, but I like to look at what other people get - look in through windows and the like. I thought I'd sleep right through it this year."

He shed his coat and ratty shoes - they hadn't found anything in his size in Luiza's closet - and crawled into bed.

Feeling oddly worse having heard that, James grunted and turned towards the fire. "Good then," he muttered. "Glad you're happy."

"I am," Sebastian said, but his tone was wistful. And a few minutes later, the tenor of his breathing told the vampire that he was asleep.

Silence descended on the room, broken only by the crackle of the flames. It was soothing, and Grim settled deeper into the chair, allowing himself to be hypnotized by the ancient dance of the fire over the logs. It filled his vision with the twisting, leaping riot of red, orange and yellow.

After a time, he heard a sound. It was a metallic rattle, followed by a soft slide and thump, like the footstep of someone trying to be silent. But no person could sneak up on a vampire who wasn't asleep.

But the door's locked, passed through James' mind even as he got to his feet and swung around, his hand on the butt of one of his pistols. Only that fact stopped him from drawing, since the only person who could be walking around was Sebastian.

Then he drew anyway, since Sebastian was still asleep in the bed and a tall, angular figure stood poised over him, back bent and hands out to curl around the boy's shoulders.

"Get the fuck away from him," James snarled.

The pale face that looked up at him made him cock the gun, even as he felt like he'd been punched in the stomach. *What the...what the fuck?*"

"Jacob?" he whispered in a strangled voice. "You're dead."

The vampire glided towards him, lips spreading to reveal sharp canines. Jacob Marley was exactly as he had been the last time James had seen him, over four hundred years before. The same long buttoned coat. The same straight hair caught in a tail and falling to his waist, black as a moonless night. The same pale blue eyes, like icicles in his sun-starved, sallow face.

The only difference were the chains wrapped around him. His body was bowed with them, and they rattled with every step.

The window had bars, and the door was still locked. How had he gotten in?

"Yes, James," Jacob hissed. "I am dead, thanks to you. I was a monster, like you, and now I'm a ghost, trapped between life and death for eternity."

James felt the temperature drop in the room. Sebastian shifted restlessly, and his breath steamed. So the chill wasn't just from the memories this face was bringing flooding back to him.

"We're both trapped between life and death," James growled, pointing the gun straight at his old friend's forehead. "We're vampires."

Jacob shook his head. "Once I was proud, vital, so alive," he said, his voice wracked with longing. "You know what I mean - how alive you feel when the blood slides over your tongue. Now I hunger, every night, and I can never quench my thirst." He raised his hand, and it passed right through the muzzle of James' gun, leaving a rim of frost on the barrel.

"Mother of Jesus!" James hissed, stumbling back a step in his surprise. His back hit the mantel of the fireplace and he froze, realizing he was liable to step right back into the fire if he moved back any further. "What in God's name are you?" He rarely took the Lord's name in vain, and the words burned his tongue as they escaped his lips. But he was so startled, he barely noticed.

Jacob lowered his hand, his mouth pulling down sorrowfully. "I know it's hard for you to hear this, James, but I've been sent here to warn you. You have to believe me when I say that I am dead."

James hesitated, then lowered the muzzle of his gun. "Say what you have to say," he said. He was sure that if his heart could beat, it would be beating a hole in his chest. He would have thought he was merely dreaming, but it was so vivid! He couldn't quite convince himself that a dream was all it was.

Jacob sighed softly. "So proud, as always," he said. "James, tonight you will be visited by three ghosts. They are the Ghosts of Christmas Past, of Christmas Present, and of Christmas Yet to Be. You *must* listen to them, or great disaster will visit you before the start of the new year." James felt the chill as the ghost moved closer, Jacob's face looming huge in his vision.

Jacob's deep voice shivered through him like a drumbeat. "And when you walk the earth as a ghost, your chains will be heavier than mine. Your endless hunger will be even fiercer! Please, my friend, you must change your ways. You must not remain a monster."

James wanted to step back, but there was nowhere to go. In a near-panic, he shoved away from the mantel, and felt a deep, soul-chilling cold as he passed right through the apparition. "This is madness!" he hissed, moving into the middle of the room as he pointed the gun at Jacob. He tried to tell himself that his hand wasn't shaking.

"We were young when you and I met. We killed hundreds together. But I've changed! I hunt monsters like we used to be - like you were when I killed you!" James cried, forgetting that Sebastian lay sleeping only a few feet away.

Jacob shook his head and drifted backwards. The rattle of the chains was loud and discordant in James' ears. "The fact that you believe you've become righteous only shows how far you've sunk. How deep you've fallen. Please James...don't make the same mistake I did."

The ghost passed into the fireplace, sinking right into the wall. James leaped forward on impulse, reaching with his free hand even as Jacob grew translucent and began to fade. "Wait, Jacob!"

* * *

James jerked awake with the suddenness of a slap

to the face, almost leaping right out of his chair. He looked around wildly, the wisps of the dream still clinging to him. But there was no rim of frost on the wall, no chill in the air. In fact, even though the fire had begun to dim, the room was quite comfortable, even toasty.

He let out a breath, sinking back against the back of the chair. So it had been nothing but a dream after all, and he'd gotten so worked up about it! If he'd actually hopped up to follow Jacob, he probably would have dived right into the fire.

A clock tower tolled nearby and James jumped again. Whispering a curse, he rose and moved to the window in time to see half the city out on the streets, all headed in the same direction. The bells were tolling midnight, but he could hear the ringing of church bells as well. Midnight Mass.

Well, good for them.

Then he heard someone clear their throat, and whirled to face an intruder for the second time that night.

This time, the figure wasn't someone that James recognized. It was a woman, dressed in flowing white robes that put James in mind of a bishop's accoutrements. The gun was jerked from its holster instinctively, but he didn't actually cock it. What in hell was going on here?

The woman was tall and willowy, her face seeming somehow at once youthful and incredibly aged, though James couldn't put his finger on why. Blonde hair spilled from under a tall white hat, and James wondered if perhaps that was what made him think of Catholic bishops. There was a kind of glow about her that made her stand out in the darkened room, as if she was lit from within.

"Who the hell are you?" James greeted her. He was sick and tired of this weird night already, and it was probably all a dream, anyway. Sebastian still slept soundly, despite his raised voice.

She moved towards him on feet so light James had to look down sharply to see if she was actually touching the floor. "I am the Ghost of Christmas Past," she said. Her voice was dulcet, a pleasant contralto that made James' mouth water. But he smelled no blood, only dust and ash, and the heat from the fire.

He lowered the gun and holstered it, watching her warily. "So you're one of the ones Jacob warned me about," he said. "Well I'm not going to play your games, lady. Get going."

She smiled and shook her head sadly. "I'm sorry, James. I can't do that. But I'm only here to show you some things. Surely you can indulge me."

He felt her slim hand slip into his own and stiffened. He hadn't intended to let her come so close. Her fingers were so slender, they felt like brittle twigs in his hand. Or maybe icicles. There was none of the warmth of life in her body.

He sighed. It was only a dream, anyway, though it felt *so* real. What was the harm? "Fine," he growled. "Show me what you have to show me."

Nothing happened, and yet the world changed around him. He felt a wash of dizziness come over him as the room whirled in a shifting kaleidoscope of colour, though he felt like he was standing on a floor as solid as a rock. The cold hand of the ghost felt as solid as ever in his, and he felt himself squeezing tightly as it went on. She didn't make a sound, and the bones didn't break under his fingers.

Then it all stopped, and he looked around in confusion. It was another bedroom, much like the hotel room he had just come from, and it was vaguely familiar. "What is--"

"James, come look at these figures for me, will you?" At the sound, James whirled around, completely forgetting about the ghost as her fingers slipped from his hand. The voice was all-too familiar, a voice that had commanded instant obedience, as well as respect.

His father sat at a desk surrounded by a pool of lamplight, papers spread all over. He had James' dark hair, though it was neatly trimmed and quite short. An equally neat beard adorned his chin. His fingers were slender like the vampire's, stained with ink from the very ledgers he was writing in.

James took a startled half-step forward, but then felt as much as saw a shadow pass by. He caught a glimpse of another figure moving towards his father and made a soft choking sound in his throat.

It was him.

The other James was twenty years old, the spitting image of himself now, centuries later.

But that made sense, because James had just realized exactly where he was. Alexander Grim had been a successful merchant, and travelled all over Europe plying his trade. By this time, both his wife and son frequently joined him on his travels, as the young James began to learn the art of trade so as to one day inherit the company.

James had loathed figures and charts, but had been a fair shake at negotiations. Beautiful as his mother, and more charismatic than his bookish father, James had quickly learned how to make a deal that was favourable to both sides, especially himself. It had even earned rare praise from the older Grim.

In Prague, they had stumbled upon some undervalued merchandise. They had rented this townhouse, and James had brokered a deal with the merchant that he hoped would bring them a substantial profit. But that profit would never be realized.

He whirled to face the ghost as the two Grims, father and son, bent over the figures. "Why did you bring me here?" he demanded.

The ghost only smiled with that same sorrowful look in her eyes. "Just watch," she whispered.

"They can't hear me, can they?" James asked as he turned back to watch himself. He saw the ghost shake her head out of the corner of his eye.

"Look, they're right!" the younger James suddenly exploded, slamming his fist down on the table with such force that a pen clattered to the floor. "I've gone over those figures three times. I can't find the problem, but it's close enough. What's the difference?"

"Son, you're not looking closely enough," Alexander Grim's voice was calm, but growing more and more impatient. "You need to learn to attend to details. God is in the details."

"Why doesn't anyone ever look at the big picture?" James snapped. "That's what's really important. Who cares if it's a penny off when you make thousands of Euros? It doesn't matter!"

"It does matter--"

The door slammed open and James the younger walked out, grabbing his coat as he went by. Despite a growing unease, the older James hurried after him, down the steps, and out into the swirling winter night.

A few drunks stumbled past them on their way back from some Christmas party or another, but for the most part the streets were deserted, locked up tight against the dark. There was a blizzard, and it was bitter cold, but the younger James only pulled his coat closer around himself and huddled in the doorway.

Unwilling to go forward, unwilling to go back.

A red jewel flared in the young man's cupped hands as he lit a cigarette. He smoked it, and James watched himself calm down. But the vampire's unease only grew.

"Go inside you stupid, stubborn mule!" he shouted at himself, waving a hand in front of the young man's eyes. Young James only went on smoking, beginning to shiver.

"He can't hear you," the ghost said, her voice carrying easily over the howling wind. "You can't change the past, James."

James rounded on her, stalking towards her and shaking a fist in her face. "Then why did you bring me to see this?"

"Because, you need to understand what came before," she said. Behind him, there was a cry of fear, but James didn't dare turn around. His mind's eye supplied every detail anyway. "Before you can understand what comes after."

Despite every ounce of will he could bring to bear, James turned and watched.

The vampire was cloaked in black, hood pulled down low. James had never seen his face, and the young man had already made his doomed attempt to flee. He was caught, slammed up against the icy stone wall of the townhouse.

"Delicious," the vampire mocked him, his mouth rimmed with red and teeth dripping with it.

"Stop this," James whispered, echoed by his younger self.

Neither the ghost, nor the vampire, heeded their pleas.

It was both torturous and mercifully quick. Within seconds the younger James had been drained of blood and had had a few drops of blood poured into his mouth from the slashed arm of the cloaked vampire. Moments later, the monster melted into the swirling snow, and James lay as if dead in the snowbank a few feet from the door, slowly being covered by the blanket of white.

James turned back towards the ghost. "Enough, please," he murmured, shaken. It had somehow been worse to watch than it had been to experience. Worse than any hunt he had witnessed in the centuries since.

"Enough?" the ghost replied. "Not nearly enough, James."

The world swirled around them again, but steadied quickly. Now James was standing back in the bedroom. His parents were sitting on the bed, hugging each other. His mother Elizabeth was sobbing into his father's shoulder, while the man sat stony faced and silent.

"Why?" Elizabeth sobbed. Even in her grief she was beautiful, her crying almost an art form with the handkerchief held just so and her eyes glimmering with tears. "Why did he go out at night? What did you say to him!"

"I had no idea he could be so rash," Alexander whispered. The blood was gone from his face, but his eyes were still dry. "But Elizabeth, he could be alive. He might have just spent the night somewhere and will return today."

"It's almost dusk," Elizabeth spat, shoving herself away from her husband and pointing a trembling finger towards the window. "Why would he have taken so long? You know he has to be dead, Alex!"

"Liza--"

James stared in growing horror. He had never seen this, of course, but his mother's alternate grief and wrath, and his father's stoicism didn't surprise him.

What did surprise him was how strongly they truly felt for him.

Grief welled up inside him as he heard the desperate pounding at the door. He heard his own voice. "Mother! Father! Please let me in!"

"James!" Elizabeth exclaimed, jumping to her feet. "Oh James!"

"Elizabeth!" Alexander cried. He reached for her, but his fingers caught only air as James' mother flew down the stairs and threw open the door. James ran as if pulled inexorably in her wake and Alexander thumped down the stairs behind them.

The young man on the stoop was covered in snow and his coat was wrapped tightly around himself. He was shivering and his lips were blue from the cold. "M-Mother, I'm s-sorry. I spent the night in a b-barn. I..."

"Oh my *darling* boy," Elizabeth cried, reaching for him. "You can't believe how much we worried about you."

"Mother, no!" Shouted James to no avail, but he could hear his own father's voice even louder.

"Elizabeth, get away from him!" Alexander cried. But it was too late.

The distraught woman reached for her beloved son and wrapped her arms around his slender and shaking form. The embrace drew him over the threshold.

"Thank you, mother," the young man whispered.

And with one bite, he tore her throat out.

Blood fountained and the brand new vampire drank thirstily. James stood helplessly in the middle of the stairs, staring in horror as the blood painted the walls and stained his mother's beautiful lavender dress. He was aware of his father staring in equal horror right behind him, but the watcher didn't turn, didn't even try to tell him to run.

There was nowhere to go, and it was too late for him, anyway.

James was aware that he was shaking, but he couldn't tear his eyes away. His younger self drank his fill, and then looked up, animal lust in his eyes as he gazed up the stairs, through the invisible James, and right at his father.

"Father, did you grieve for me?" the monster whispered with gory lips.

"Yes, son," Alexander said softly. "As I do still."

There was a blur, almost too fast even for James to follow, and the vampire was on Alexander. The man went down without even a cry.

He hadn't even tried to escape.

James turned to his left and saw the ghost standing there, watching the carnage with impassive eyes. "Please ghost," he pleaded, hating himself for the display of weakness, but unable to bear this any longer. "I've put this behind me. I'm not a monster like this anymore. Why are you torturing me with this?"

She turned to him, and the world swirled again. "Have you really put it behind you?" she asked.

The smacking sounds of the monster drinking Alexander Grim's blood disappeared, but was replaced with the screams of a young blond woman he and Jacob had taken turns with one night. It had taken her hours to die.

James closed his eyes and covered his ears. "Stop this!" he screamed. "I've changed! I'm not like this anymore! Stop this now!"

The sounds changed again, to a more masculine tenor of scream. James didn't open his eyes, afraid to recognize the face of another victim.

Even more terrified that he wouldn't recognize him, that he was just one of a parade of hundreds that he'd killed and forgotten.

"Changed, have you?" the ghost whispered in his ear as the screams disappeared, replaced by the patter of running feet. James struck out towards the voice, but hit nothing. Despite himself, he saw the scene now in front of him.

Jacob Marley fled down an alley, and was

confronted by a high stone wall. He turned, hissing, his teeth bared and sharp. "Why are you doing this, James?" he cried. James could see that he was injured, limping. Wounds such as that would close quickly, but not quickly enough. "We've been partners for a hundred years!"

Two sets of feet hurried down the alley towards the vampire. James was in the lead, his own fangs bared. In the hunter's eyes, the older James saw a lust he had seen before.

It was the same lust James had displayed right before he had slaughtered his parents.

Stunned by the realization, James watched in silence as he stalked down the alley towards his former friend. "I'm different now," the younger vampire growled. "I'm not a monster anymore."

"You'll always be a monster," Jacob hissed. "Don't you remember? The hunts we had? The kills we made!" He reached towards James, his blood-streaked hand trembling. "Don't be afraid, James. We'll rule Hell together, whatever that God soldier says."

The third man was dressed in white robes, a crucifix clutched in his hands. He had the zeal of true faith in his eyes and it was hard to tell from the way he was holding the crucifix who he was protecting himself from. Probably both of them. "Strike, James!" the priest exclaimed. "Strike now, before he tempts you!"

James couldn't avert his gaze as his younger self plunged the stake deep into his friend's heart.

Jacob fell to the ground, and the younger James allowed the stake to fall from nerveless fingers. Were those white flakes snow, or was Jacob already beginning to turn to ash? James was finally able to turn away, and he saw the ghost standing beside him, watching the scene impassively. "Enough. Please," he whispered.

"As you wish."

* * *

James awakened with a jerk. The single toll of the clock tower outside his window was still reverberating in his ears. It was one o'clock, and it had all been a dream after all.

He let out a sigh of relief and rose to his feet, turning to check on Sebastian. Given how vivid the dream had been, he imagined he had to have been tossing and turning at the very least, if not crying out. He hoped he hadn't disturbed the young shape shifter, especially since he wasn't particularly interested in explaining himself.

There was someone in the bed with Sebastian.

They were under the blanket, the larger man covering the boy with his body. The intruder was only visible as a mass of dark hair from behind. James heard Sebastian cry out in fear - a sound he was well-acquainted with - and saw the larger figure flash fangs just before biting down into Sebastian's throat.

Another cry, and by this point James was seeing red.

He hissed territorially, like a cat, and sprinted across the room. He reached out to tear the monster from Sebastian. "Get the fuck off him you--"

His hand passed right through.

"No..." James whispered, a horrible realization coming to him. The vampire lifted his head at that moment and James saw his own face, lips red with Sebastian's blood.

James took a few hasty steps back, looking around for the ghost. It wasn't over, after all. Was he still caught in the dream?

Sebastian was in the bed, but he was also standing at the window. The boy smiled when their eyes met, cloudy grey eyes bright with warmth. "Hello James," he said. "I am the Ghost of Christmas Present."

James couldn't have said he was surprised by this point. "So, the second of three is here to torture me," he growled, trying to ignore the sounds of passion from behind him. Sebastian was making soft whimpering sounds in the back of his throat.

James had come to enjoy hearing those noises over the last few weeks, but now they sounded like fear, rather than desire. Had they always sounded like that?

The ghost's smile widened. "Not to torture you, James. We're here to help you. And what could be nicer, but to watch you with your lover engaged in beautiful lovemaking?"

Wincing at the sarcasm James was sure he could hear, he found himself turning to watch again, sensing as much as seeing Sebastian walk up to stand beside him. The blanket had fallen down and there was nothing left to the imagination.

They made a good pair, and for a moment James almost wanted to smile. He himself didn't actually look much older than Sebastian, though he was considerably taller and muscled. Even still, James was slender, while Sebastian was just plain underfed. He looked small and vulnerable in Grim's grasp, and the vampire's mouth watered at the sight of Sebastian's pale face and reddened mouth, opened in an 'O' as he gasped with pleasure.

Grim thrust two fingers deep into the boy's body and Sebastian cried out again. This time it didn't sound afraid and James began to relax. Sure, he sometimes lost control over himself and bit Sebastian, but it wasn't every time, and the boy seemed to be all right with it.

If he really had a problem with it, he'd leave, after all. James wasn't forcing him to stick with him - it was Sebastian who had insisted on staying, following him around for weeks and then insisting he was going to be his sidekick or something.

Then, as Grim shifted forward, sliding his cock deep into Sebastian's body, the boy slipped his arms around the vampire's neck. Moaning deep in his throat with pleasure, Sebastian leaned up to kiss him.

Grim turned his face away from the kiss, grabbing the boy by the shoulders and pushing him back down again. "Stop that," he growled, giving a harder thrust with his hips that brought another cry to Sebastian's lips.

The watcher swallowed faintly, feeling a faint swell of shame inside him - which wasn't helped when the ghost standing beside him clucked his tongue. "Not too nice, are you?"

"No one ever said I was nice," James said, though without much heat. He folded his arms and glared at the passionate scene in front of him as the pace of the thrusts increased. Grim bit at Sebastian's skin again and again as he thrust mercilessly, holding the boy's arms down against the bed.

Sebastian writhed and cried out, and James could hear both pain and pleasure in the boy's sounds, both fear and passion. *Why does he put up with this?* James thought in growing dismay as he watched small bloody flowers blooming all over the boy's chest and throat.

"No, no one ever said that," the ghost agreed.

James glanced at him sharply as the two lovers moved to their near-simultaneous completion, Sebastian's cries peaking as ecstasy won out over the discomfort he was certainly feeling. "I have a question for you, ghost," James said.

The ghost glanced at him, eyebrows rising towards his sandy-coloured hairline. "Ask away, James. I'll answer if I can."

James clenched his fists against his upper arms, his eyes narrowing. The sounds from the bed had quieted and he paid them no mind. "How can you stand here and pretend to be Sebastian? Sebastian's not dead - he's right over there. This whole thing you've been showing me happened last night. So you can't possibly be Sebastian."

The ghost laughed. It was so much like Sebastian's bright, cheerful laugh that it was almost painful to hear. "You're right, I'm not Sebastian," he said. "But I thought this form might please you. How about this?" In a blink, Jacob Marley was standing before him, not bound in chains, but strong and vital and fairly glowing with a recent feeding.

"Or does this ease your mind more?" Suddenly he was a tall, willowy man, glowing white from within.

James didn't recognize this one.

Then he was Sebastian again, grinning up at James cheekily. "Does it really matter what I look like?"

"I guess not," James muttered.

Sebastian was disentangling himself from the covers and Grim's tired grasp. "Where are you going, kid?" Grim asked irritably, catching the boy by the hand.

Sebastian just turned to smile at him. "Just going to clean up a bit James. I'll be right back."

Grim grunted something noncommittal and withdrew his hand, and Sebastian went into the small water closet adjoining the room, closing the door behind him.

To James' surprise, he found himself following the boy. He passed right through the door and found the boy leaning on the washbasin, his eyes shut tightly, his breathing rapid and shallow.

"What's wrong with him?" James exclaimed in concern, reaching for the boy's shoulder, but again it passed right through with no reaction.

"What do you think, James?" the ghost asked softly. In stark contrast to his attitude thus far, his voice had shifted into a sorrowful tone.

With shaking hands, the boy wet a towel and began to rub at the wounds all over his chest, arms and neck. Thanks to James' vampire saliva, most of the small bites were already closed, leaving nothing behind but a bit of blood. Sebastian winced as he scrubbed at the blood on his still-healing throat.

Suddenly James saw Sebastian in a way he had never seen him before. He saw the weakness, the pallor he had always assumed was simply a hold-over from the boy's hard life on the streets. And now he understood that it was the pale skin of a boy under too much strain as the blood servant of an over-demanding vampire.

It made him feel sick to his stomach.

Sebastian dropped the bloody towel into the basin, swayed and caught himself, then sank to the floor in a graceless motion.

Half-kneeling, half sitting on the floor, Sebastian covered his eyes with his hands and began to shake in earnest.

James felt a knife stab into his heart as he watched, but this time he didn't even try to turn away. "Does he do this every time?" he whispered, almost to himself.

"Maybe, maybe not," the ghost said. "Do you really need me to tell you?"

There was no need to answer that question. James turned to the ghost, swallowing a lump of horror in his throat. "Why does he stay then? Why does he do this to himself? I'm not forcing him to stay--" doubt forced him to add, "--am I?"

"Why don't you keep watching," the ghost said as Sebastian finally picked himself up off the floor. "And see if you can figure it out for yourself."

James couldn't argue with that. He watched as Sebastian rinsed out the towel as best he could, squeezing pink water out of the rough terry-cloth and hanging it up again. Then he leaned on the basin for a moment, as if girding himself for some task.

After a few seconds, he straightened, and James saw a bright smile spread across his face as Sebastian stepped out of the water closet and moved back towards the bed. "All done," he said brightly, hopping into bed with Grim once again. The vampire muttered and tugging him close, but to James' new perspective, he saw that the gesture was far more possessive than affectionate.

But it was what James had seen in Sebastian's eyes that left him speechless.

In those blue eyes, so familiar to him and so naked, he had seen love.

More than that, and most damning, James had seen hope.

Hope that James would soon come to appreciate him for more than a light snack and fuck before bedtime? Or maybe hope that one day, James would simply start to treat him like a human being, if he was just cheerful enough, compliant enough, loyal enough.

James was crushed by shame. "What have I done?" he whispered. "Dear Lord, what am I doing?" The words were close enough to a prayer that they blistered his lips.

The lamps were dimming, and the bed seemed suddenly far away, hard to see in the growing darkness. Outside, somewhere distant, the clock struck two o'clock.

"Ghost," James said, turning to look for the faintly glowing boy. "Ghost please, what do I do now?"

But there was no one there. James turned in a circle, feeling a cold wind stir his hair and coat. There was no hotel room, no uneasy lovers nestled in an embrace.

He was standing in a graveyard.

The wind whipped up and its chill sliced right through James' coat. Though he hadn't been much bothered by the cold in hundreds of years, he pulled his collar up and close around his face.

"What the hell is this?" he muttered. He couldn't recall ever being in this particular cemetery before, though after a few thousand zombie killings in a lifetime, one boneyard started to look pretty much like another.

A soft exhalation of breath made him turn around. It seemed to drop the temperature another ten degrees and a flurry of snow blasted him in the face as he turned. He shivered, and drew his coat even more closely around himself, but it was futile.

The sound was like the death rattle of a person so aged that you could barely tell they were alive to start with. It came from a heavily cloaked and hunched person, so swathed in black clothing that James could barely make out a human figure under all the layers.

It raised a hand, which was bared to the cold, blue-veined and liver-spotted, and beckoned James nearer.

Wary after the hellish night he'd already had, James moved closer. "The Ghost of Christmas Yet to Be?" he said. "You're here to show me my future?"

The figure seemed to nod. It turned and pointed, and James saw a gravestone ahead. The earth freshly turned and piled beside the gaping hole that had been dug.

Swallowing faintly, James moved closer, leaving the ghost behind.

The grave was empty, just a deep, yawning black hole barely penetrated by what little light could penetrate the clouds. Belatedly, James realized that it was day, but the clouds were thick, the flat, iron grey of snow. A blizzard would be coming soon; he could smell its crisp scent.

James bent slightly, trying to see the letters on the stone, but it was blank except for three letters - R.I.P. *Doesn't anyone know whose grave this is?* he wondered. Well, at least it didn't bear his own name.

Not that anyone would bury a vampire.

The sound of approaching footsteps made him look up and he saw two men wheeling a small cart up the path. A body was sprawled in the cart, covered by a sheet. It looked rather small and forlorn. The men were moving quickly, taking turns pushing and blowing on their hands. They obviously wanted this unpleasant business done with.

"No one here to see this one off, eh?" one of them said as they approached the grave. "Not that I can blame 'em, what with the storm coming."

"Nope, not a one. Hear he was just staying in that hotel in town the last few days. Was found dead in his room this morning."

"So he's a traveller then. No passport? No one he was with?" The first speaker seemed concerned, but in a vague way that told James he'd forget about it immediately once the subject was gone from his sight.

"Some say he arrived with someone, stayed with him, but he just up and left in the middle of the night. Probably killed the poor bastard and ran before he could be caught," said the second man, taking a moment from his labours to turn to one side and spit.

He then leaned closer to his companion. James

strained to hear his next words, which were spoken in a conspiratorial tone. "Heard tell that there was a lot of screaming coming from that room."

The cart was wheeled right up to the edge of the hole. As one, the two men each grabbed one of the handles and tipped upwards. The body slid from its cradle and fell with a heavy thump, and as it fell, the shroud slipped from the face of the corpse.

James leaped forward with a cry, nearly jumping right down into the grave itself. He dropped to his knees and bent down, straining to catch another glimpse of the face he had seen.

Perhaps it was a lucky gap in the clouds, or James' vampiric night sight, but he could easily see Sebastian's waxy, pale face down at the bottom of the hole. The boy's eyes were closed, and his face had a peaceful expression. But the dark, angry tear of an unhealed vampire bite stood out starkly on his throat.

The two men saw it, too, and they crossed themselves in unison. "You think a vampire really got into the hotel?" the first man said. "Isn't it protected?"

"Are you stupid? A vampire can get in if you *invite* them," the second man scoffed. "And this boy, he obviously invited him in, if you catch my meaning. I hear there was a party going on when they arrived. Lucky they aren't all dead."

"Gotta burn this one before he rises," the first one commented. They were already unloading packs from their backs and setting them down. The contents were obviously heavy and sloshed. Lighter fluid, no doubt.

James was barely listening anymore. He sat at the edge of the grave, hands covering his face. So he was a monster after all, except that he'd chosen to give this boy - who deserved none of it, whose only crime had been poor judgement - a slow, lingering and painful death instead of the quick ones he'd given so many others.

A skeletal hand touched his shoulder and he looked up into the shrouded face. "Isn't there anything I can do to stop this from happening?" he pleaded. "Is this future set in stone?"

The wraith shook its head, and pointed to the grave. The men were pouring lighter fluid down over the corpse of James' lover.

The lover he would kill.

"No!" James hissed. He jumped to his feet, clenching his fists. "I won't accept this! Sebastian deserves better than this. I'm not going to kill him!"

He turned his back on the ghost. Somewhere, he thought he heard a clock tolling. Three bells? Four? He couldn't quite hear.

He strode away from the grave. "The future isn't set," he growled, as much to himself as to the ghost. "I won't let this happen. I'll change things, right now. Release me!"

* * *

Sebastian awoke with a start, though it took a few moments for him to figure out what it was that had awakened him. He sat up, running a hand through his unruly sandy hair and peering through the darkness towards the chair set in front of the fire. The back of the chair was tall and wide, but he could see a bit of James' arm poking out. Was he still sitting there after all this time, or had he gone out for the night and just returned?

It was quite dark in the room. The fire had been allowed to die down to nothing but glowing embers and dawn was still a ways away.

Not that far away, though. Even from the bed, Sebastian could see the sky had turned the deep purplish black colour of predawn.

That meant...it was Christmas.

There was a winter chill in the room that the sad remains of the fire couldn't hope to combat, but Sebastian stole out of the warm protection of his covers anyway. Today, for the first time since his family had been killed and he'd been left to fend for himself, he would be truly able to enjoy Christmas. Sure, he wasn't expecting presents, but he would be warm and safe. Maybe James would even be willing to give him a *little* money, so he could get himself something.

A Christmas cake, maybe. That would be nice.

Sebastian's toes curled as they touched the cold wooden floor, and he tiptoed across the room to the window. He leaned against the windowsill looking out, but there was no one yet up and about. Soon the sun would start to come up and he would have to close the curtains to protect his friend from the sun.

And while James slept, Sebastian would go out and enjoy the day. It was hard to contain his excitement.

He heard James shift in the chair, and a soft exhalation, and that spurred Sebastian to turn. "James!" he exclaimed, but then stopped in surprise. The vampire was slumped in the chair, asleep. Why was the vampire asleep in the middle of the night?

But Sebastian's voice startled James out of his doze and he jerked upright. "What? Sebastian!" he exclaimed, looking around in startlement. When he saw Sebastian, his eyes softened with…relief? But why?

Sebastian moved away from the window, putting aside his confusion in favour of his enthusiasm. "It's almost Christmas morning, James. I wonder if people got presents. Did you really sleep all night?"

James rose from his chair hastily. Outside, a clock began to ring six...no, seven chimes. Sebastian beamed, the sun would be coming up in less than half an hour.

"I...yes, I slept," James said, shaking his head in a confused manner. Sebastian gazed at him perplexedly. What was wrong with him?

"Are you all right, James?" Sebastian asked uncertainly. "You're acting weird."

James opened his mouth, but seemed to think better of whatever he'd been about to say. "I'm going out," he said abruptly, turning away and striding towards the door. On the way, he grabbed his hat.

"What? You can't go out now, James," Sebastian exclaimed. The sun was about to come up, how could he think of going out? "What's wrong?"

"Don't go anywhere," James ordered him sharply. "I'll be back." He opened the door and paused, then glanced back. The expression on James' face made Sebastian's jaw drop - he looked...concerned, and kind. There was a reassuring smile that played about his lips. "Don't worry, kid. I will be back soon."

And with that he was gone, leaving Sebastian with his jaw still on the floor.

A moment later, Sebastian pulled himself together enough to rush to the window. He caught a glimpse of a dark figure exiting the inn and hurrying down the street. Where could he be going?

And why hadn't he let Sebastian come with him?

Could he be leaving for good? Despite the front that Sebastian struggled to maintain, he was well aware that James had been reluctant to bring him along. That was why he had followed the vampire for weeks instead of simply asking to travel with him.

If he were going to run off, he wouldn't do it now, Sebastian told himself. *He could have left when I fell asleep. Now he'll have to hole up somewhere until dawn.*

But then...what is he doing? Is he sick?

That seemed far more likely. Why else would a vampire sleep the night away and then run recklessly outside right before dawn?

Worry rose up and nearly choked him, and Sebastian murmured a quick prayer that James would come back before dawn, safe and sound. Maybe God had forsaken vampires, but Sebastian still held onto a kernel of hope that He'd make an exception in this case.

But dawn came and the sun rose, the first rays setting the snow blanketing the ground and the roofs of the buildings to sparkle. Sebastian paced back and forth in front of the window, then finally left off to build up the fire again. But even though he added enough logs to build it to a merry crackle, the warmth couldn't penetrate the ice in his stomach.

If James were going to come back, he should have done it by now. Now Sebastian certainly wouldn't see him again until evening.

He was going to have to spend Christmas alone. Again. Somehow it hadn't seemed so lonely to know that James would be asleep for the whole thing, but now that he was *gone*, it was a whole different thing.

Sebastian curled up in the chair where James had spent the night, wrapped in a blanket and staring into the fire. He could hear banging and chatter downstairs and smelled frying bacon. He closed his eyes and burrowed deeper into the blankets. All around the city, children were waking up and tearing open presents, exclaiming over their new toys and laughing. Parents were yawning and making themselves coffee, and exchanging their gifts while their children were still up to their elbows in paper.

But there was none of that for Sebastian. He didn't even want to go out and watch, like he'd originally planned.

Suddenly the door banged open. James burst into the room, but threw up an arm to shield his face with a loud hiss. "Shut the goddamn curtains! What's wrong with you?" Was it Sebastian's imagination, or was smoke rising from James' body?

Stunned, Sebastian merely obeyed. He scrambled from the chair and darted over to the window, pulling the curtains closed and cutting off the light of the sun.

He turned, his heart pounding from surprise, and a bit of fright. What was going on? "James! Where did you go? Why did you--"

"Stop asking questions!" James snapped, and Sebastian closed his mouth uncertainly, chewing on his lower lip.

James took a deep breath and ran a hand over his

face. There were some red patches on his skin - burns? - but he paid them no mind, pulling off his hat and coat and casting them aside. "I'm sorry," James said awkwardly. "I shouldn't have yelled at you. It was...it's day."

Sebastian let out the breath he'd been holding in a loud exhalation. "Well, *yeah*," he exclaimed, throwing up his hands. "You scared me to death, James, going out like that!"

The vampire wasn't looking at him. Sebastian felt a frown furrow his own forehead as he watched the older man. He'd never seen him acting even remotely like this, and it worried him all over again.

He moved across the room, and caught James' hand, startling the vampire into meeting his eyes. "Let's sit," Sebastian said gently, gesturing towards the bed. "Then maybe you can tell me what's gotten into you this morning."

"Yes -- no!" James said, tugging his hand free and picking up his coat again. For a horrible second, Sebastian thought he was going to throw it on and leave again, but he was just rooting through the pockets. "I have to - here, this is for you."

A small box was shoved so suddenly and unexpectedly into Sebastian's hands that the boy nearly dropped it.

The box was wrapped hastily, a few corners sticking out and the tape askew. There were no bows, and no label, but it was a present.

And it was for him.

Sebastian's knees went weak and he sat down on the side of the bed quickly for fear that he would fall. "For...me?"

James shifted from foot to foot. "I...forgot to get you a present before," he said. "And it's hard to get things like that at night anyway. None of the stores are open."

The mattress shifted and sagged as James sat down next to Sebastian. There was a long silence, before James shifted uncomfortably. "Aren't you going to open it?" he prompted.

That broke the spell just enough that Sebastian recalled himself to what he was doing. Right, yes. You *opened* presents. You didn't just stare at them in utter shock. He looked up at James, feeling a brilliant smile spread across his face. "You really got me a present."

"Looks like I did," James said, impatience beginning to edge his voice. "Are you going to open it or not?"

"Of course I am," Sebastian said, glancing down at the brightly-wrapped object in his hands. "I guess I..." he laughed, high and bright. "...I want to savour the moment."

"Stop savouring and start opening," James growled, but there was a grin on his face. *He's as excited as I am,* Sebastian realized, and he beamed fiercely, grabbing the wrapping paper in both hands and tearing it from the box.

Inside was a gold bracelet, set with a single blue stone. The solid gold band was cut with an interesting geometric design. Sebastian stared at it in utter shock and amazement. Something so expensive and extravagant - just for him!

He floundered, picking up the precious piece of jewellery and turning it over in his hand. "James, I...I can't accept something like this!"

"What are you talking about?" James exclaimed. "Why not? What's wrong with it?"

"Well I...it...it's so expensive..." Sebastian stammered.

"Hogwash," James growled. "You'll accept it and you'll wear it. Money isn't the issue."

Sebastian swallowed. "But..."

"It's not just a piece of frippery, you know. Let me show you," James went on, ignoring him and snatching bracelet right out of Sebastian's hand.

He pressed his thumb down on the gem, then dropped the bracelet with a hiss and a short bout of swearing.

Startled, Sebastian bent down and looked at the bracelet. All over it, little bits of metal had popped out, each one in the shape of a tiny cross. It now looked more like a charm bracelet than the solid piece it had been before.

"An anti-vampire bracelet?" Sebastian breathed, bending down to pick it up. James leaned away a little and Sebastian quickly started snapping the little crosses back into place.

"Yeah," James said. "Everyone knows about crosses, and vampires know how to get around them. But no one'll expect that. If you keep hanging around with me, you'll meet all kinds of vampires who aren't gonna be as nice to you as I am."

His lips thinned. "And you don't hesitate to use them on me if you need to. Got it?"

Sebastian shook his head, slipping the bracelet over his wrist. "There's no need. I know you lose control sometimes, James, but I trust you. You'll never go too far."

James opened his mouth, clearly intending to object, but Sebastian leaned over and locked his arms around the vampire's neck, silencing him with a soft kiss. "Just accept it, James," he whispered. "You can't get rid of me that easily."

With a soft, rueful chuckle, James wrapped his arms around Sebastian's waist and tugged him into his lap. "So it seems. Well, the bracelet is just the first step in coming to terms with that, I guess."

"Exactly," Sebastian said with a grin, and settled his head on James' shoulder. Finally...it was finally happening. He could relax now. James wasn't going to push him away after all.

But then a horrible thought struck him. "James," Sebastian said, glancing up with sudden horror. "I didn't get you anything!"

James smiled, and Sebastian felt his arms tighten around him. "That's okay," the vampire murmured. "I don't need anything from you I don't already get."

Then his expression turned a bit sly. "Well, except maybe more of this." He ducked his head down and stole a gentle, but passionate kiss - the first of many they shared on that bright Christmas morning.

Grim Hunt

The hard shaft was smooth in Sebastian's hand and a bit slick as he shifted his grip. He switched hands and rubbed his palm down his thigh.

"You nervous?"

James Grim's voice was soft, but he spoke nearly into Sebastian's ear, nearly making the boy jump out of his skin. Hot breath tickled his earlobe.

"No," he lied, his voice a little high and strained.

James chuckled softly and only confirmed to Sebastian that he wasn't hiding his fear very well.

"Good," James said. "There's nothing to be afraid of, kid. I'll be right there with you all the way. You trust me, right?"

At that, Sebastian smiled faintly and turned, giving James a quick kiss. The vampire grumbled, but ruffled Sebastian's hair affectionately all the same and he found himself relaxing.

"Of course I trust you. Is it time yet? Can we do it now?"

James glanced over his shoulder. "Sun's coming up. It's about time."

Sebastian shifted the wooden stake back into his right hand and nodded. "I'm ready. Let's kill some vampires."

James chuckled again and slipped past him, out of the alley where they'd been waiting and over to the doorway of the little house on the opposite side of the street. Sebastian followed closely, his heart in his throat and his hands sweating and turning the stake slick once again.

A light snow was falling from the sky and their feet left fresh prints in the sugar coating on the cobblestone street. The air was January crisp, enhancing the absolute silence all around them. Sebastian couldn't even hear a single dog bark, or the small noises of early risers.

He wasn't surprised by that, but it still heightened his tension.

The neighbourhood was all but abandoned, houses left empty for blocks in all directions. Most people could do nothing about a vampire infestation in their midst and often had no choice but to move out rather than rely on the thin protections of garlic and faith.

That was why the Vatican employed vampire hunters like James Grim. The fact that James was also a vampire himself mattered little, so long as the infestation was dealt with decisively and with as little collateral damage as possible. Sebastian had long ago recognized that while James had a monster inside him, James himself was a good man.

The trouble was convincing James of that.

Sebastian had been following James around Europe ever since the hunter rescued him from a vampire nest in France, but it was only recently that the vampire started to look at him as less of an inconvenient hanger-on and more of a companion. He had even - finally - begun to train him.

Tonight was his first real lesson. Apparently it was going to be trial by fire. Literally, if things got out of hand and James had to use the accelerant he'd hidden in one of the many pockets of his long black coat.

They had arrived at the door and James reached for the knob. It was locked, of course, and the vampire grunted with displeasure. "Time to look for a window to break," he said. "They'll be in the basement, probably, so we just have to hope they don't hear."

"What if they do hear?" Sebastian asked, reaching out to catch the sleeve of James' coat before the taller man could head away.

"Well, then things could get interesting," James said wryly. "But don't worry, I do this all the time."

Sebastian grinned and let go of James' sleeve. "How about we do something different this time?" he suggested. Under James' disbelieving gaze, he fished a couple of twisted pieces of wire out of his pocket and went to work on the lock. It was a simple thing, and soon it disengaged with a click.

James made a soft, surprised noise, and Sebastian grinned, opening the door and letting it swing open with a faint creaking sound.

"Where did you learn to do that?" James whispered, moving past Sebastian again and through the doorway.

"The same place I learned to pick pockets,"

Sebastian whispered back. "All part of trying not to starve on the streets."

That earned a grunt from James and they moved through the house in search of a door to the cellar.

The stairs down to the basement creaked under James' weight. Following James down the rickety steps, Sebastian winced at every sound. His hand crept upwards and curled around his mother's cross, hanging as always from its chain around his neck. The vampire-repelling bracelets James had given him for Christmas were a comforting weight around both wrists, as well.

Soon they had reached the floor of the basement. It was hard-packed dirt, smooth and dry and a little soft under Sebastian's shoes. It was pitch black, and Sebastian stared around nervously for a moment before an impatient noise from James reminded him that they'd anticipated this. Quickly, he fumbled for the small hand-lamp he'd secreted in his pocket.

A moment later the small halogen flashlight illuminated a small wine cellar. The racks of wine had been removed, and replaced by four large wooden boxes. Four coffins.

Four vampires.

"I thought there were only two," Sebastian whispered, near panic. The light reflected on the curved, polished surface of the lids. They were a dark mahogany, seeming almost to absorb the light and return only a pittance.

"Keep cool," James said sharply. He reached into his coat and pulled out a stake. "If we do this fast, they'll never know what hit them. I can handle this many. If you want to go back up and wait, it's fine."

James' doubts dismissed Sebastian's panic better than any reassurance could. He pushed the terror aside and firmed his grip on the stake. "No," he said grimly. "I can do this, James. Please don't send me upstairs."

The vampire turned and gave him a long, searching look, his eyes glittering in the light from the flashlight. Of course, alone James wouldn't have any need of such a thing. But Sebastian was only human.

A special human - a shapeshifter - but human nonetheless.

"Okay," James said finally. "You go to that end, and work your way towards me. We each take two. Be quick."

Brightening, Sebastian darted to the far left coffin, while James walked over to the far right. Sebastian set the flashlight down on the floor, turned upwards to illuminate the area and approached the coffin.

Now was the moment. Sebastian's heart hammered in his chest as he reached out and lifted the lid of the coffin. It moved easily, without a single squeak in the well-oiled hinges.

The interior was lined with satin, a crisp white that glowed under the flashlight. The vampire in the coffin looked like a fresh, preserved corpse, resting in perfect repose. He had been young when he contracted the virus, and long lashes rested against cheeks that had never felt the touch of a razor.

Some part of Sebastian's brain reminded him sharply to be quick and he lifted the stake, bringing it down to rest over the other boy's heart. He retrieved the hammer hanging from his belt, and tested it against the stake, preparing to strike.

Then, for the space of a few heartbeats, he hesitated. *Vampires are evil. I've always hated them, ever since they killed my parents,* he thought, staring down at the waxy face of the young vampire. He looked the same age as he was, still in his teens.

But James isn't like that.

This nest is so vicious it's caused everyone in three blocks to flee their homes!

From across the room, there was a horrific crunching sound as James drove a wooden stake through the chest of a vampire. Still Sebastian stared at the stake in his own hand, watched the tip dimple the vampire's skin.

But he's so young. What if he's just being forced? What if he just doesn't know how to act like a person instead of a monster?

Sebastian realized gradually that the vampire's eyes were open. His heart nearly stopped as their eyes met.

"Uh..."

That was all he got out before a hand shot up out of the coffin and clamped into the collar of his shirt. The vampire twisted hard, and tugged Sebastian downwards, and he realized that he couldn't breathe.

The stake slipped out of Sebastian's grip as he struggled, clattering to the floor. He reached for his cross, but it was fouled in his shirt, caught under the fabric and impossible to pull out as long as the vampire had a grip on his collar. His lips moved, but no cries for help emerged. He could feel the blood pounding in his ears and saw the vampire's mouth open, the fangs poised to strike.

Sebastian raised the hammer and struck almost

blindly at the vampire, but with a flick of a hand, the vampire knocked Sebastian's hand aside before it could connect. Black sparks were beginning to flash across Sebastian's vision and so far as he could tell James had no idea that anything was wrong. The open lid of the coffin cut off his view of the rest of the room.

Then a memory of James' words came back to him. *" Everyone knows about crosses, and vampires know how to get around them. But no one'll expect that."*

Mouth open in a soundless scream of terror, Sebastian brought one hand around to the other and pushed in the gems on both bracelets. Tiny bits of metal in the shape of crosses popped out of the seemingly solid gold bracelets, and he desperately pressed his wrists against the arm of the vampire.

The sizzling sound of cooking flesh was overwhelmed by the loud hiss of pain as the vampire released him. Sebastian threw himself backwards in panic and a jolt went through his body as he landed on his rump on the dirt floor. Miraculously, he still had his hammer in his hand, and the flashlight hadn't been knocked over.

"Kid! Are you okay over there?" James exclaimed, then there was a smack and a grunt of pain. Sebastian couldn't see what was happening, but it sounded like James had run into troubles of his own.

The young vampire Sebastian had been hesitating over killing was sitting up in the coffin. He looked a bit groggy, shaking his head, and the spots on his arms where the small metal crosses had touched him were an angry red.

He turned to look down at Sebastian on the floor and smiled as he started to climb out of the coffin.

Sebastian scooted away another few inches and hit a wall. The stone was hard and cold against his back, even through the coat he was wearing. "L-look, I know you're really mad," he said, his voice coming out as a croak from the abuse his throat had taken. "I understand. I do. But it doesn't have to be like this."

The sounds of battle went on at the other side of the room, but on this side of the coffin, Sebastian and his vampire were in their own little world. Somehow, even the gunshot that rang out a moment later seemed far away. Maybe it was because it was so hard to hear over the sound of Sebastian's heart beating a mile a minute.

"What doesn't have to be like this?" the vampire asked, stepping out of the coffin and dropping to his knees in a graceful, liquid motion.

"We don't have to kill each other," Sebastian said desperately. "Did they just turn you? You don't *have* to be a monster, you know. The other guy over there - he's a vampire, too. He's good, like he was when he was human. You can do it, too!"

The vampire stared at him for a few moments, then threw back his head and laughed. "Oh you little morsel. You're very new at this, aren't you?"

Sebastian could feel the rest of his blood draining out of his face at the chilling sound of that laughter. "M-my first real hunt," he admitted softly.

The vampire began to crawl towards Sebastian, taking his time. "Then you should know that I am not what you think in the romantic corners of your heart, child. I am over three hundred years old. If I ever wanted to stop being a monster, the time is long past for that."

He touched Sebastian's ankle and the shapeshifter pulled it back with a squeal of fear, drawing his knees up to his chest.

"The three children your friend is killing are only a few of those I've created," the vampire purred. "And perhaps, if you are very lucky, you'll be next. Of course, you'll die with the others at the hands of your friend, and I'll be long gone."

"Th-the sun..." Sebastian whimpered. The vampire was so close now, he could feel his hot breath on his face.

"You really think I'm that stupid?" the vampire whispered. "I have an escape route planned, of course. Unlike you, I am not that young and foolish."

As the vampire leaned in for the kill, something broke inside of Sebastian. *No,* he thought, with a sudden clarity. *Not again.*

Grabbing the chain of his cross, he drew it up out of his shirt in a single motion, and punched the vampire in the throat with it clenched in his fist.

The sharp edges of the cross dug into his palm as the punch connected, but the vampire flew back as if it had been struck by a sledgehammer. Sebastian sprang forward before he could stop to think about what he was doing. He snatched up the stake from the floor as the vampire slumped against the side of the coffin and drove it as hard as he could against the vampire's chest.

Drawing back his other arm, he slammed the hammer into the head of the stake as hard as he could.

If he'd thought about doing it, it would never have worked. Somehow, the hammer connected perfectly, and the sharpened stake punched straight through the vampire's breastbone and into his heart.

The vampire gave a loud shriek, then seemed to wilt, his eyes closing with a kind of finality. A drift of ash sifted from his face and slowly the entire body seemed to fold in on itself as it began to disintegrate.

Gasping for breath, horrified at what he'd done and still feeling the after-effects of terror, Sebastian climbed shakily to his feet.

Then someone came at him out of the dark and he raised the hammer with a scream.

"Sebastian!" James grabbed his wrist, then instantly let go with a hiss of pain.

It snapped him out of it, though, and Sebastian blinked stupidly at his friend. "James? What happened? Is it over?" he asked, hearing the tremble in his own voice.

"It's over. I got the other three while you were dealing with this one," James said, nodding.

"Oh thank the Lord and Jesus," Sebastian prayed, seeing James flinch. The hammer dropped from his nerveless fingers and he crumpled to his knees on the floor.

James was down next to him in an instant. "Hey, hey are you okay?" the older man asked worriedly. Sebastian could scarcely hear him through his relief.

Maybe I'm not cut out for this, he thought. The thought made him want to burst into tears. He rubbed his face, and his hand came away wet, but not with water. He stared for a moment, realizing that blood had sprayed from the vampire when he staked him, and he hadn't even noticed.

"I'm sorry," he whispered. "That was so bad."

James laughed softly. "You did better than I did the first time, kid. You killed it - that's the important thing."

Sebastian forced himself to turn his head and look at what was left of the vampire he'd killed. It really *seemed* like an 'it' now, just a drift of ash and some clothes. He really had been pretty old, like he said.

"Really? You let the first one get away?"

"Well, not the *first* one," James said, and there was an odd note in his voice. "But I've let some get away, sure. Shit happens. Come on, let's get out of here."

Despite his words, James didn't reach for him as he normally might have, either to pull him to his feet or simply urge him to move faster. Sebastian wondered if it was because he was bristling with gold crosses, or if James was worried how he'd react if he was touched.

Feeling guilty, he looked down and began pushing the little crosses back into his bracelets.

"Sebastian," James said, his tone growing more urgent. "You don't have to worry about that now. They're dead. We can leave."

"Hush," Sebastian murmured, popping the last one into place. With a feeling akin to reverence, he lifted the cross hanging around his neck and slipped it back into his shirt.

Then he turned and threw himself into James' arms.

James made a yelping sound in surprise, catching him easily, but rocking back with the force of the impact. "Hey!" he exclaimed, but Sebastian didn't let him get anything more out.

With a desperation that was completely uncontrolled, Sebastian sought James' lips with his own. He kissed the older man so hard he could feel the shape of James' fangs through their lips, wrapping his arms around James' neck and clinging with all he was worth.

James was stiff for a moment, startled, but it wasn't long before he returned the kiss with a sharp, possessive growl.

Sebastian felt himself being borne to the floor as James thrust his tongue into his mouth. He sucked on it gladly, spreading his legs for James to slide between them. He didn't care that this was a bit sick - that the body of the monster he'd just killed was lying only inches away.

Somehow, this was what he wanted. What he desperately, so desperately, needed.

And it seemed James wanted it just as badly.

James pulled back slightly and Sebastian lifted up, making a soft noise of need as he sought another kiss. James gripped his shoulders and pushed him back down to the floor. "Did it hurt you?" he asked, his voice a low rumble of barely-leashed anger.

Sebastian shook his head quickly. "No, he didn't get the chance. Please, James."

"Good," James murmured. "I didn't think I could smell your blood amidst his stink. But I wasn't sure."

For a moment, Sebastian was horror-struck all over again. Had the vampire done something to make him undesirable?

Then James lowered his head again, but instead of

kissing him, his tongue flickered against Sebastian's cheek. Sebastian held very still as James cleaned the blood from his face in a way that was both disturbingly animalistic and at the same time possessive and strangely erotic.

Before James was quite done, Sebastian's hands began to wander. He unzipped James' fly and drew his member from his pants, stroking it to full hardness. There wasn't much he needed to do. Almost at the first touch, James' cock swelled and lengthened to full arousal, hard and hot in Sebastian's hand.

James growled, nuzzling against Sebastian's neck. His teeth scraped, but didn't break the skin. "You really want to do that here?"

Despite his question, the older man's hands were tugging at Sebastian's clothing, opening his fly and pulling at the waistband of his pants. Sebastian lifted his hips to help him.

"Yes," Sebastian pleaded softly, his fingers pulling harder at James' cock. "I don't care where. Just please, do it."

"You don't have to fucking beg," James muttered, but Sebastian could hear the pleasure in his voice regardless.

"I know," Sebastian whispered, smiling as fangs prickled lightly against his skin again.

James almost always bitched and moaned, but Sebastian had been travelling with James long enough now to know what he liked. It was always such a fine line to walk, but Sebastian was getting better at it, and James hadn't been biting him nearly as often since Christmas.

Stripped of his pants, Sebastian spread his legs

even wider, drawing his knees up slightly.

"Christ in heaven," James said. "We don't even *have* anything, kid. I don't keep lube in my goddamned pockets when I'm hunting--"

"Don't stop," Sebastian begged. "Please."

Giving a put-upon noise, James lifted his head long enough to stick two of his fingers into his mouth. The fingers went in stained with red and came out shiny with saliva. It was a poor substitute for lubricant, but Sebastian couldn't care less.

"Don't say I didn't warn you," James said softly, then wormed both fingers deep into Sebastian's body.

Despite his best efforts, Sebastian couldn't stop a soft whimper of discomfort from escaping his lips. He reached up with his free hand and curled his fingers in James' long black hair, pulling him back down into a kiss as he squirmed and his body took its sweet time in adjusting.

And for all of James' worry, it was clear he wasn't any more inclined to wait than Sebastian was. Long before Sebastian had fully relaxed, James pulled his fingers free and shifted until his cock was pressing hard against his entrance. Sebastian squeezed his eyes shut tight, taking short, sharp breaths as he struggled to relax. James bit hard at Sebastian's lips, drawing blood and then kissing him deeply and hungrily as he pushed slowly into Sebastian's body.

The pain was deep and intense for a moment. For a moment, it seemed they had gone too fast, and Sebastian cried out as it peaked. Then it began to ease and Sebastian realized that James had stopped, buried deep inside him. He trembled, stretched to the breaking point, as James literally feasted on his lips and waited impatiently for Sebastian to relax.

It seemed to take forever, but finally Sebastian forced himself to nod. "Do it," he whispered. "I'm okay."

The first thrust was almost as painful as the original penetration, but the pain swiftly diminished as his body stretched to accommodate James' girth and precome slicked the passage just enough to ease the friction to bearable levels. Soon the sharp, pained breaths coming from Sebastian's chest transformed to rapid pants of pleasure and he clawed at James' back, rocking up into each thrust.

James slipped a hand between them, stroking Sebastian's cock hard and fast.

"You...Sebastian..." the vampire murmured as the pace of his thrusts increased and Sebastian writhed helplessly on the packed dirt floor.

"W-what?" Sebastian gasped, opening his eyes and looking up at James. The vampire's eyes were closed, his eyebrows pinched in concentration.

Then James opened his eyes. "You're mine," he growled. "And I'll kill anyone who tries to take you like it tried to take you."

Sebastian's mind reeled, and all he could do was nod in confused acceptance. "Yours," he gasped.

James bucked against him, grunting aloud as he climaxed. The pace of his stroking hand increased, and Sebastian cried out helplessly, the odd exchange flying right out of his head as his own orgasm hit him almost out of nowhere.

Pleasure slammed through his body and he clung hard to James as they both rocked together to their completion. As the waves crested and subsided,

Sebastian collapsed to the floor bonelessly, gasping for air.

He only lay there for a moment, however, before James wrapped his arms around him and pulled him up and against his chest. Still impaled on James' softening cock, Sebastian found himself sitting straight up, his head tucked under James' chin.

"James?" Sebastian whispered when he could speak.

The only response was a wordless grunt.

Sebastian opened his mouth a few times, discarding a few possibilities. But what did you say?

Did you really mean it when you said I was yours?

What does that mean, anyway?

Finally he just shook his head and relaxed against the older man. "Nothing."

All he really knew was that, whatever James had meant, it made him feel safe. To Sebastian, it meant that he belonged.

A Note from the Author

Hi readers!

I'm Jessica Steiner, but when I'm writing the Grim stories, I write under the pseudonym of Suzanne Fisher. While I love writing about James Grim and Sebastian, I also write full length fantasy and science fiction novels. At the time I'm releasing this story, I've released one novel, *Mortis Unbound*, and I'm pleased to include a sample here, in case it tickles your fancy.

If you're interested in staying plugged in with any new releases, or seeing what else I'm up to, please check out my blog and join my mailing list. You can do both at http://jessicasteinerbooks.com.

And now, please enjoy the first chapter of *Mortis Unbound*.

Mortis Unbound
A Fantasy by Jessica Steiner

Laxamora, 316 A.B. (After Breakthrough)

Mortis heard the banging, felt the swaying, even in her dreams. It angered her, and she hammered futilely against the interior of her prison. The impacts of her own fists echoed in her ears, assaulted her senses, and did nothing. *Nothing.*

Sleep tried to drag her down again and she prepared to surrender. Nothing she did mattered, and she would never escape. It was better to live in dreams.

But then she heard shouting, a *"Be careful with that!"* and a jolt ran through the prison.

Then she sensed it: the tiniest of hairline fractures in the glass. It was too small to see, but for her, it was enough.

She burst from her imprisonment and rose into the air in a shower of glass, wings unfurling. There were humans all around her, men and women who wanted to put her back in the prison. She wouldn't let them. She wouldn't go back to that endless hell.

She spread her hands and the humans were falling, dying, their little lives snuffed out effortlessly. She felt nothing except the relief that they could not hurt her again.

Her feet touched the ground once more, when the last human lay dead on the floor. They lay all around her, like broken matchsticks and of just as little consequence. Glass sliced into her feet. Pain, strange and foreign and unpleasant, jolted through her body like tiny bolts of lightning.

She wanted to escape. Needed to hide, but she didn't know where to go. Where could she hide?

She stepped over one of the bodies.

The certainty she had felt was fading, subsumed by fear and memories of the endless sleep. She pressed her hands to her eyes, shuddering. Where could she go? Who was she running from? That didn't matter. What mattered was that she was running, and she was all alone in the world.

She straightened. She wasn't all alone. There was one person. He might be an enemy, but he was the only person in all the world whose face she could picture in her mind. Everything before that quickly became smothered in fog. If he was an enemy she would do...do something.

She would not go back to prison.

Death could find anyone. She stumbled out into the street, gavoxae tugging at her hair with their little hands, and savoxae wrapping their chill arms around her, toying with her skin.

She turned towards the place where she knew he could be found, and took flight.